CRIME
and
PARCHMENT

Daphne Silver

CRIME
and
PARCHMENT

A Rare Books Cozy Mystery

DAPHNE SILVER

LEVEL
BEST BOOKS

First published by Level Best Books 2023

This novel is entirely a work of fiction. The names, characters and incidents portrayed in it are the work of the author's imagination. Any resemblance to actual persons, living or dead, events or localities is entirely coincidental.

Daphne Silver asserts the moral right to be identified as the author of this work.

Author Photo Credit: Debi Spencer-Zerby

First edition

ISBN: 978-1-68512-508-0

Cover art by Level Best Designs

This book was professionally typeset on Reedsy.
Find out more at reedsy.com

Dedicated to my mom Brenda for instilling in me a passion for reading, writing, and creativity. May this finally give you the robin's egg blue Karmann-Ghia you always wanted.

Praise for Crime and Parchment

"I love the way Daphne Silver twists fact and fiction together in *Crime and Parchment* to create a unique mystery involving the covers for the *Book of Kells*. I can't wait to see what happens next in this charming, new series featuring rare books librarian Juniper Blume."—Sherry Harris, Agatha Award-nominated author of the Sarah Winston Garage Sale and Chloe Jackson Sea Glass Saloon mysteries

"*Crime and Parchment* sends its readers on an exciting mix of history, small town secrets, romance, and murder in this captivating start to a wonderful new series!"—Emmie Caldwell, national bestselling author of the Craft Fair Knitters Mysteries

"I've rarely been as intrigued by a cozy mystery as I was while reading Daphne Silver's *Crime and Parchment*. The debut novel in Silver's Rare Books series combines well-researched history with fictional elements to deliver a fascinating mystery. The search is on in the Chesapeake Bay town of Rose Mallow for the priceless long-lost covers to the sacred 9th-century *Book of Kells*. Who better to investigate than rare books librarian Juniper Blume, especially after she literally stumbles across the body of a murdered woman while planning to meet about the missing covers with her estranged brother-in-law who has now disappeared? With a diverse cast of characters, heartwarming relationships, and a unique bayside town full of charm and history, this cozy version of National Treasure will keep readers enthralled and waiting impatiently for Juniper's next Rare Books adventure."—Korina Moss, Agatha Award-winning author of the Cheese Shop Mystery series

Chapter One

My 1965 robin's egg blue convertible backfired as I parked in front of the Wildflower Inn. The noise set off Clover barking in the backseat. Not exactly the quiet homecoming I'd hoped for. I jumped out of my Karmann Ghia—or "KG" as I'd nicknamed her—to check under the hood, hoping I wouldn't need to get the roadster serviced yet again. No idea where that money would come from.

A screaming, ranting madwoman poured out of a neighboring house. Maybe in her late seventies, she brandished a large umbrella. I dropped the hood to find the umbrella pointing at me. Clover—all twenty pounds of him—jumped out and started growling.

"Easy, boy," I said.

"You shoot something off, Missy? Here to cause trouble? Because I'm on the board of the Friends of the Rose Mallow Police." the woman said. She wore a perfectly fitted Mamie Eisenhower pink skirt suit with enormous pearls—straight out of the 1950s. Her white bouffant billowed around her head. She reminded me of a researcher I'd helped earlier that day at the Library of Congress. That woman had been a murder mystery author looking for books about early detectives. This woman looked like she wanted to murder someone—namely me.

Suddenly, I remembered her: Cordelia Sullivan. She was my late grandmother's arch-nemesis. After my Nana Z had moved to Rose Mallow, they'd competed to be the president of almost every board in town. Nana Z had called it a "friendly rivalry to garner the most civic goodwill," but I don't think Cordelia saw it that way. To her, the Blume family were—and always

1

would be—outsiders in her perfect Chesapeake Bay town.

"What's going on?" My sister Azalea appeared on the wraparound porch of the Wildflower Inn. Although I was two years younger at twenty-eight, she looked like my twin, except that her hair was much longer and darker than my slanted bob. She pushed her bangs back and brought a hand up to her forehead when she saw me. "Juniper? What on earth are you doing here?"

"Well, I…." My words faltered. I'd spent the past hour driving and trying to figure out how to tell Azalea about why I'd finally returned, but every time I tested the words out loud, they failed. Clover had listened with confused curiosity before giving up and falling asleep.

"You know there's a noise ordinance," Cordelia said as she waved her umbrella around. Clover barked at the offending instrument. However, I think he wanted to play with it more than anything else. Occasional growling aside, he's not exactly attack dog material.

"Yes, Mrs. Sullivan. Not until ten p.m., and it's not even eight o'clock yet." Azalea's exasperated voice led me to suspect that she'd had this conversation more than once.

"Hmph. I plan on taking your 'halfway house' to the zoning board. What a travesty to do to our pristine historic district. You know I'm president of the Rose Mallow Historical Society." Cordelia wagged a finger at my sister. I closed my eyes before rolling them.

"Mama! Mama!" A young bundle of legs and a mop of nearly black hair appeared next to Azalea on the wraparound porch. I couldn't believe how big Violet had grown. She was almost four years old now.

She latched onto Azalea's legs and held on tightly. I wanted to run up to my niece and smother her in hugs and kisses, but I wasn't sure how I'd be received. Clover apparently did, too, because he took off after her. The little girl squealed with laughter as he covered her in licks.

"Go inside, Vi. It's past your bedtime," Azalea said. She turned to us. "I don't have time for this. As you can see, I have a young child requiring my attention. Plus, I have a house full of guests. Mrs. Sullivan, it sounds like you have a plan in place to handle my zoning and noise issues. I'll leave you to it. And Juniper, if you're here, then let's get you inside."

Violet ran inside, letting Clover follow. I took that as a positive sign, so I grabbed my suitcase from the trunk and followed quickly, as Cordelia monitored us. Her umbrella remained held out in the air. She reminded me of Don Quixote in pearls.

"You've done an incredible job restoring the place," I said as I walked across the perfectly manicured lawn. Azalea had recently converted Nana Z's Queen Anne-style mansion into a boutique hotel. After so many years away, I hadn't been sure what to expect.

She eyed me with uncertainty. I could tell she was debating whether to chew me out for not being here for any of the work, let alone the hotel's grand opening earlier in the spring. But my sister is much better at maturity than I am.

"It's been a journey. Not an undertaking for the faint of heart. Repairing that turret alone had me almost give up and put up the for sale sign." Azalea pointed up to the three-story round tower protruding from the side of the house. As a kid, I used to pretend Nana Z's home was a castle and fought many dragons racing up that tower.

"You wouldn't."

"I said 'Almost,'" she replied with a laugh.

"I love how bright the yellow siding is. I bet that color really pops in the morning against the Chesapeake Bay." I walked up the stairs to the wraparound, past garden beds bursting with purple coneflowers and Black-Eyed Susans, Maryland's state flower.

"You know what's funny is how much I hated canary yellow when we were little. Every time we came here, I'd always wished Nana Z's house was more like Cordelia Sullivan's with her dark greens and rich reds. But now that Nana Z's gone, I couldn't stand to change it," Azalea said.

"But it's such a cheery color. Why would you want something so drab as Cordelia's place? " I asked. As a kid, Cordelia's house had been as scary as the owner. Losing a ball into her yard meant it was never coming back. Neighborhood kids claimed her house was haunted.

Azalea shrugged. "Yeah, the yellow's growing on me."

"You kept this mess?" I said when I spotted the clunky clay mezuzah on the doorpost. I'd made the case at Jewish day camp as a kid. Inside was a tiny parchment scroll inscribed with biblical verses in Hebrew. The painted clay design was supposed to be a bunch of zinnias in honor of Nana Z's first name, but it looked more like a lumpy mud puddle than a bright firework of flowers.

Azalea shrugged with a smile. "Oh, there are a few of my own masterpieces on some of the other doors inside. Maybe I'll get Violet to make some new ones."

The inside was as exquisite as the outside. I don't think my memories did the place justice. The stained glass above the front door also sported Black-Eyed Susans, while those above each window featured a different native wildflower.

Azalea had kept our grandmother's lush red carpets with ornate gold and white floral patterns. Polished mahogany inset panels gleamed from the walls. A staircase with beautifully carved spindles fed into the large lobby.

On the left was a parlor that Azalea had turned into the registration space. On the right was the library, overflowing with leather-bound books. It was in this room I had discovered my love for stories and books as a child. I wouldn't have become a rare books librarian at The Library of Congress without Nana Z's library. I sighed, wishing things were going better there. Nana Z would have been proud of me, but my job had become so difficult since I lost that promotion to Greyson. A little birdie had told me not to expect another chance for a long time, which meant I was stuck with someone Nana Z would have described as a "schlemiel."

A narrow hallway disappeared between the registration area and the staircase, which led back to the dining room and kitchen. I remembered how those overlooked the back garden, public boardwalk, and the Chesapeake Bay. I could imagine how ornately she'd decorated the upstairs bedrooms.

Clover sniffed at everything in sight. I monitored him, but he was having a grand time exploring. Just not too grand of a time. I tried sending the message to him telepathically. He lifted his nose at me as if to say, "Who, me?"

"I love that you hung some of Nana Z's watercolors," I said. My eyes grew misty as I gazed at her paintings of native flowers, including dwarf crested irises, ironweed, columbine, and, of course, the rose mallow for which the Maryland town was named. I shook my head, pushing the grief down deep.

A teenager hunched over a thick book sat at the registration desk. She had long, bluish-green locs that looked beautiful against her sepia-brown skin. Her large glasses were rimmed in a matching turquoise color. She looked up from the book and said, "Sorry, Azalea. Vi got away from me."

The teen didn't seem alarmed, but then again, neither did Azalea. I wondered if this happened frequently. Maybe Vi was a regular escape artist. Nana Z would have been pleased. I held back my smile.

"I'm Juniper, Azalea's sister," I said to the teen as I extended my hand.

"You have a sister?" she asked Azalea with a look of surprise. Then she recovered, shook my hand, and said, "I'm Keisha Douglass. I've been helping Azalea with the Wildflower Inn. But, uh, we're all booked up tonight."

"I'll figure it out," said Azalea. "Although giving me some sort of a heads up you were finally coming would've been nice, Juniper."

I didn't know what to say, so I smiled awkwardly. Clover raced over to the desk to check out Keisha. The desk was higher than him, so he couldn't quite see atop. Fortunately, she came around to pet him. "Oh wow! A dog? We're allowing dogs now?"

I turned to check with Azalea, who massaged her temples. She breathed deeply but then simply shrugged. Great. Not only had I shown up out of the blue, but I hadn't checked to make sure pets were allowed. I was pretty sure I knew the root cause of her sudden headache. I smiled sheepishly.

"No worries, Keisha. Clover's the exception to the no-dogs rule. Vi's fine. I'm going to put her to bed," Azalea said as she ushered the bouncing kid down the narrow hallway and turned abruptly right before the kitchen. Unsure of what to do, I followed. There was a small sitting room there, which she had reconfigured into a bedroom. It was a tight space. Azalea caught me staring. "It's a temporary solution. I'm still working on updating the Carriage House in the back garden. Once I'm finished, Vi and I will move there."

Vi ran around the room, fighting Azalea's attempts to return her to bed. My sister paused mid-chase and said, "This may take a bit. You know where the kitchen is. Why don't you go there, start a kettle of tea, and I'll meet you there when we're done? I was getting ready to pull a kugel out of the oven anyway."

That was my sister, always gently commanding, whether it was an unruly neighbor, an energetic preschooler, or me, the surprise guest. I thought of her like a duck. Above the water, she appeared to be smoothly sailing along, but below, it was a mad fury of management to keep everything afloat.

"A kugel?" I asked with excitement. Nana Z had made plenty of the baked noodle casseroles each summer. Sometimes, they were savory, but more often, they were sweet, made with lokshen, or egg noodles, and various cheeses.

Azalea looked pleased. "I've been trying to perfect her recipe. You'll have to tell me what you think."

I knew immediately she meant Nana Z. As we headed down the hallway, I caught the aroma of the decadent noodle pudding. I could already detect the cinnamon she'd used. My eyes watered slightly at the memories the smell produced.

The kitchen was both familiar and new. No longer was it the 1890s meets 1970s chic that Nana Z had employed. Azalea had replaced most of the yellowed appliances with updated stainless steel, upgraded the laminate countertops to granite, and removed the harvest gold wallpaper to paint the in vogue "greige" along with a matching subway tile backsplash. Someone had been watching a lot of HGTV. But it was still Nana Z's kettle on the stovetop, her handcrafted cookie jar on the counter, and a variety of favorite teas in the same cabinet location. Being here felt like being at home, but only if that home had been completely renovated when you weren't looking.

The view out back remained the same, looking past a blooming garden of blue hydrangeas and the small Carriage House, to the public boardwalk separating the garden from the Chesapeake Bay. On good days, you could make out the shoreline on the Eastern Shore. Being early June, the sun was beginning to set beyond the Bay's edge, so the view became a Tonalist painting with its atmospheric blues, grays, and browns.

Clover found an embroidered tea towel to play with. I tried pulling it away from him, but he decided that meant the game was afoot. I dug into my suitcase and found his food. I borrowed a couple of low rimmed bowls to fill with his dinner and water. He quickly abandoned the towel for something to eat.

According to the timer, the kugel still had a few minutes left in the oven. I caught the kettle before it whistled and filled up two mugs. Given the abundance of Darjeeling black tea, I assumed it was still Azalea's favorite and prepped it for both of us. Within a few minutes, she came in, plopped down on an empty seat, and dropped her head to the table. I sat up in alarm, afraid that my cool-as-nails sister might be about to cry.

"Why are you here, Juniper? Why now?" She didn't look up as she spoke. She cradled her head in her folded arms. Unsure of what to say, I gingerly placed my hand on her shoulders. I was amazed when she didn't swat it away. I pressed into her shoulder and could feel her sob.

"How'd you know? How did you know I couldn't do this all on my own anymore? Divorce is even harder than I had expected. And it's not like I thought it'd be a walk in the park, but it's so much worse." She sat up, tears streaming, and leaned over to me, pulling me into a firm embrace. I hadn't known what to expect returning here, but it certainly wasn't this. However, I wouldn't turn her warmth down. I debated about how to tell her the truth about why I'd finally come back to Rose Mallow.

While my sister and I were close in age, we had never been close in person. She was the logical-minded entrepreneur, while I was the pie-in-the-sky academic dreamer. I don't think Azalea had ever not toed the line. I'd never seen her speed or take an extra sample from the grocery store. Sure, we shared a love for anything old. I loved books and clothes, and she couldn't resist an antique store. Restoring Nana Z's house must have been a dream project for her, combining a love for all her passions. I wouldn't be surprised if she had measured everything personally or drawn all the blueprints.

"Uh, excuse me." A young man with a goatee interrupted our tender moment. "But we need more toilet paper in the…. What's it called? The Forget-Me-Not Room?" He started laughing. "Oh, that's funny that I forgot the Forget-Me-Not. That's right, right?" That phrasing set off another burst of laughter. He didn't seem to notice or care that neither of us had joined in his amusement.

"Sure, I'll be there in a moment. Do you need anything else?" Azalea turned on a dime. She was all sunshine and smiles. You'd never know she just confessed her pain to me a moment ago. She was gone for about half a minute before returning. "Teenagers."

"He didn't look like a teenager."

Azalea shook her head. "I meant Keisha. She should have taken care of him. Look, she's amazing, but she gets so caught up in her books sometimes. And if it's not her books, then it's her latest coding project on her laptop. I constantly have to remind her that she's at work, not at a study session."

"Oh, like when Violet ran outside?" I remembered the brief exchange when we had come into the inn. Azalea nodded in agreement.

The timer for the oven went off. Clover looked up, startled at the sound. Azalea got up, grabbed some oven mitts, and pulled the kugel out of the oven, placing the casserole dish on a trivet to cool. Out of the oven, I could get even more scents. If I wasn't wrong, she'd added apples and raisins to it. Clover noticed, too, pacing below the counter. He whined, obviously hoping someone would give him some.

"Not now, Clover," I said quietly to him. He tilted his head to the side before giving up and returning to his food bowl.

"But Keisha's fabulous. She got our website up and set up our reservation system. Plus, she does all our social media. And she responds to every online review. She can get a bit distracted, which is not great when we have a packed house," Azalea said as she returned to the kitchen table. The kugel would need time to cool. She added some honey to her tea and offered me some, which I accepted. The jar looked like it was from a local farm. It smelled tantalizing.

"A packed house?" I remembered Keisha saying that there weren't any rooms. Were Clover and I going to need another place to stay tonight? Not to make it all about us, but it was a consideration floating through my mind. Besides, it's not like I had asked about staying. Nope. I had just shown up and expected my dog and me to be welcomed like royalty. I gulped at my tea, hoping I seemed less inconsiderate in real life than I did in my head.

"You ever watch that show, *Professor Treasure Hunter?*" Azalea asked.

"Oh, him."

Azalea looked at me with confusion. She obviously hadn't expected how much my face darkened at the mention of his name. I sighed and explained, "Last year, Orson Bradford – your so-called 'Professor Treasure Hunter'—had been a speaker at the Society of Rare Book Librarians conference. Sure, he was more into popular history than my more erudite colleagues, but he was at least entertaining. He was also completely drunk at the conference hotel bar when he blatantly hit on me."

"Well, okay, so he's not staying here himself," she went on, "but the entire television crew from the Chronos Channel is. And all their equipment, too. Getting around upstairs is a bit of an obstacle course. He's been doing a book tour for his new memoir."

"Right. The book's not so originally named *Professor Treasure Hunter.* He talked about it at the conference." I made a face at the memory. "But Rose Mallow? Why here?"

"They say he has some sort of announcement planned. He's staying with friends or something, but they're all here this weekend and possibly beyond. I don't know yet, but at least it's steady business. And right now, I could use all the money I can get," Azalea replied. She sipped her tea.

"Do you know what he's going to talk about?"

"Not a clue."

"For the Chronos Channel? Probably aliens or mad cow or Nazis," I said with a laugh, thinking about their typical show themes. Of course, right then was the exact moment when the goateed guy came back. He threw me a death glare. Great, now I had insulted my sister's guest. I threw my hands up in apology. He shook his head and stormed off. Fantastic. Simply fantastic.

To my surprise, Azalea just laughed. She took a generous swig of her black tea. I looked at her with concern. "How're you holding up?"

"I don't know. Some days, I think divorcing Rory was the right choice, but other days…" She sat there, looking out the back bay windows at the gardens in the back yard. I followed her gaze. Darkness descended, but I could still make out the tall shrubs and bushes, the outline of the Carriage House, and beyond to the water's edge. Increasing numbers of fireflies darted about. Summer in Maryland could be humid, but it was undoubtedly beautiful.

She stood up and headed to the kitchen counter. After pulling out two plates, she cut squares of the kugel for each of us. Clover jumped up again, but I shook my head at him. He seemed to pout but didn't race after her. Azalea sat the plates in front of us. I stared at it, wanting to dive in, but feeling tremendously guilty.

"I have to tell you something," I said. My heart pounded in my chest. I wondered if she could hear its tattoo.

"What?"

I gulped deeply. "I'm back in town because of Rory."

"What?" Azalea looked at me in surprise.

I sipped at my tea and thought of how to explain. "This afternoon, he emailed me while I was at work."

"Why on earth would he email you?" she asked.

"Have you ever heard of the *Book of Kells*?" I asked.

She looked confused. "You mean that old book in Ireland?"

I laughed despite myself. It was an understatement to call a 1,200-year-old illuminated manuscript just an "old book." Azalea gave me the stink eye, so I explained. "I saw the *Book of Kells* when the Society of Rare Book Librarians had their conference in Dublin. Beyond spectacular. One of my absolute favorite books in the entire world."

Seeing the *Book of Kells* at Trinity College in Ireland had been a high item on my bucket list. I nearly cried looking at the 9th-century masterpiece which illustrated the Gospels. Each page featured elaborate and exquisite medieval paintings with vibrant colors and brilliant gold leaf on vellum. It was larger than I had expected, and I couldn't imagine the hours—really, the years—it must have taken to create. Although Azalea and I had been raised in a culturally Jewish household, I nonetheless found the loving care of the artwork to be transcendent. *Kells* might not have been my sacred text, but it was still sacred to me.

"But why would he email about the *Book of Kells*? Rory doesn't care about books or history. Remember when I worked briefly at that antique store, and he found my work 'boring'?" Azalea asked.

"Yeah, I know. My curiosity got the best of me, so I called him." My obnoxious boss had been on my case lately, so I snuck into a cramped janitorial closet to make the call.

"What did Rory say?"

"He said he'd found the missing covers." When I heard him say that, I had assumed the smell of cleaning supplies in the tiny closet was messing with my head.

Azalea, however, looked baffled. "The covers are missing?"

"For over a thousand years. Back in 1007, the books were stolen from Kells Abbey in county Meath, Ireland. Maybe by Vikings, but I don't know. Miraculously, the manuscript was discovered months later, apparently 'under a sod,' but they were missing their original gold and jeweled cover. Folios from the start and end of the manuscript were also gone, likely destroyed when the ornamented covers had been ripped off. I'd always assumed the covers were sold or taken apart for their valuable jewels and gold. Either way, they were never seen again."

Azalea stared at me. "Okay, so these fancy covers were stolen, and Rory—my ex Rory we're talking about—found them? But he works for a car dealership. Here in Rose Mallow. In Maryland. How would he have found them? He's not an archaeologist. And, I don't think he's been out of the country before."

"I don't know. He said they're here. He promised to show me proof."

"And you believed him?" Azalea asked with a snort.

"Well, he sent me some photos."

"Of the covers?"

I grimaced. "Not exactly."

"Then of what?" she asked.

I pulled out my phone, found the photos, and handed it to my sister. She pinched and pulled at the screen, just as I had done a few hours earlier. "They're from something called the O'Doyle diary. He says it's from about 1650, although it may be earlier."

"How can you tell what this is? These are impossible to see. Is that supposed to be a picture of something? Violet can draw better than this," Azalea said.

"Yeah, the resolution's pretty awful. I think that one is a map. See, that's the Chesapeake Bay," I replied.

"If you say so."

"He asked me to come here to explain things. He promised I could look at the diary and anything else he had," I replied.

I knew how foolish it sounded, but I couldn't resist finding out more. The mere chance he might be right…. I shook my head. I knew better than to think he'd found one of the world's greatest missing literary treasures, but on the off chance it was true, that they were in Maryland. I needed to find out. It seemed worth the hour's drive south from D.C.

Azalea was quiet. She stared deep into her tea. Our kugels remained untouched on the table. Finally, she lifted her head and said, "You missed the grand opening of the hotel three months ago."

"I know, and I'm sorry," I started to say, but Azalea held a hand up to interrupt my apology.

"You never came for any of Violet's birthdays. You knew Rory and I were divorcing, and you didn't come for that."

I wanted to explain how much being here had hurt after our grandmother died, but I knew it wouldn't make any of this right. Instead, I just nodded.

"You didn't come for anything else. But you finally came back—out of the blue—for what? For some ridiculous hare-brained scheme of his? For some poorly taken photos of an old diary—one that knowing Rory is probably a fake? Really? This is what you came back for, Juniper? Not for me, not for your niece, but for some old book?" Azalea said.

I sat there with my mouth gaping, unsure of how to respond. Azalea shook her head. Her disappointment cut me deeply. I don't think I had realized how much I'd failed her until hearing her tick off my faults one by one.

"After Nana Z died, it was just too hard," I said.

"It was hard for me too," she replied.

"I know, but…" My voice trailed off. We had both been grieving, but I'd let mine eclipse every time my sister needed me. That needed to change immediately.

"There's something else you should know, Juniper."

"What?" My voice croaked.

"I've started coming home sometimes to find these, well, 'trinkets' left at my doorstep."

I didn't expect her to say that. I sat upright. "What do you mean by 'trinkets?'"

"They range. Crushed flowers. Mean notes. Torn photos of me. Things like that." Tears collected in her eyes. She looked towards the phone on the wall. "Sometimes there are breathy voicemails. No talking, just breathing. A few times, there was canned laughter. The menacing kind from the movies."

"Oh my goodness, Azalea. That's awful." I wanted to ask why she hadn't told me any of this before, but given my failings as a sister, I couldn't blame her. "Do you think they're from Rory?"

"I don't know. He's never been mean before, but maybe he thinks they're pranks. Getting some steam out. I mean, who else would they be from?" she asked.

"Wow." I had always considered Rory annoying, but I never thought him capable of stooping so low.

"But even if he just thinks he's pranking me, it's really starting to concern me. I'm thinking of getting new locks if it doesn't stop."

"Have you told the police?" I asked.

Azalea didn't answer my question. Instead, she looked me dead-on and said, "So if you're still planning to meet up with him, you should know that you're probably walking into some sort of... I don't know. Another prank, I guess. He's probably using you to mess with me. Think about it, okay?"

I nodded. "Yeah, of course."

"Look, the Carriage House is swimming in storage boxes, but if you find some place to camp out there, you and Clover are welcome to it. For tonight. Only. And then, Juniper, I want you gone."

Chapter Two

Before I could respond, a tall woman in a dark suit waltzed into the kitchen. "I've been looking for you everywhere, Mrs. Blume-Walsh." Azalea stiffened in her seat. She frosted a smile across her face and nodded politely.

"What can I do for you, Miss Collins?"

"*Ms.* Collins."

"Yes, of course. My apologies, *Ms.* Collins. What do you need?"

"It's not what I need, but what Bradford does. Twenty copies of twelve files." She held up a flash drive. She looked around the kitchen with an air of disgust. The look hardened when she spotted Clover. "I had told him I should stay somewhere with a business center."

Azalea was already leading Ms. Collins back down the hallway. "We have a great printer at the registration desk. Follow me."

I tried cleaning everything up, but I was never as good at domestic goddess stuff as Azalea, even with such a simple task. Clover danced at my feet. I glanced at the clock. It was almost eight-thirty. I hadn't told Azalea that Rory wanted to meet later tonight. After what she had said, I didn't know what to do, but I didn't feel like Azalea would appreciate it if I was still here when she returned.

After giving Clover a bathroom break in the backyard and grabbing a few more things from KG, we entered the Carriage House. It was a small cottage with a living room and kitchenette, and one tiny bedroom, although there wasn't a bed there. We navigated towers of stacked banker boxes, identified with labels like "Azalea's Books" or "Violet's Baby Clothes." I pushed stacks around, probably toppling too much over and undoubtedly breaking who knew what inside, but I managed to make space for a sleeping bag I found in a corner. I plopped the pillow for Clover beside it. He made himself comfortable and promptly fell asleep. The poor pup was wiped out after all the traveling and excitement this afternoon.

If I still planned to meet Rory, it wasn't for a few hours. Unsure of what to do next, I headed to Rose Mallow's tiny downtown area, about a mile north of the Wildflower Inn. I left Clover at the Carriage House to sleep.

Less than a hundred years ago, Rose Mallow had been a resort town on the Chesapeake Bay. People took excursion boats from Baltimore to escape the summer heat in a time before air conditioning. Others came by train for the bathhouses and beaches. The town still had its lovely boardwalk on the water, but most of the old hotels, steamboat docks, and amusement parks had been abandoned. The interpretive signs scattered across the town that told of its history were faded and peeling.

But whenever Azalea had tried convincing me to visit again, she'd talk about how there was a growing community here. Apparently, the town had recently reached 5,000 residents. She sounded hopeful that efforts to revitalize the area would attract more visitors. There was a new art center opening soon, and the historical society was leading the preservation effort to get the downtown and surrounding neighborhoods listed as a national historic district.

I found several shops on the town's tiny Main Street, all facing the public boardwalk and the Chesapeake Bay. Lots of people were waltzing between shops, taking in the late evening view of the water. Being late June, a breeze rippled across the Bay, cooling the evening air. The sun had dropped below the horizon, turning the sky black-blue with puddles of purple. A tiny sliver of pink nearly disappeared at the edge.

I stopped at the Purple Oyster Coffee Shop on the north end of the boardwalk. The Purple Oyster was part coffee shop, part bookstore, and part arts and crafts supply shop. Every surface was painted in either a vibrant shade of purple, yellow, or orange. Paintings and prints from local artists lined the walls.

"What'll you have?" asked the perky barista with purple dyed hair. Her hand-written name badge read "Tess" and was emblazoned with stickers and doodles. She was maybe twenty-two, give or take. Papering the walls were fliers for local musicians, including one that looked a lot like the barista. I spotted an empty corner spot with some chairs alongside some mics and music stands. I wondered briefly if Tess performed here.

"You match the place," I said. She looked at me curiously. I waved my hands around. "The Purple Oyster. Your purple hair. I like it. Looks really cool."

Recognition settled in over her baby blue eyes. A smile danced across her face. The boys must have been crazy for Tess. She radiated warmth. "I'd forgotten my hair was purple today. I changed it last night. Yesterday, it was emerald green."

"That probably looked just as cool," I replied.

"Excuse me. Are you going to order?" I looked over my shoulder, and my heart dropped into my stomach. Whitney Sullivan. Our neighbor Cordelia's granddaughter. I'd known her since we were teenagers. She had lived here year-round, and although we hung out with the same group of friends, I'd never been more than a "summer leech" to her.

"Hi, Whitney."

"Well, look at what the cat dragged in. Juniper Blume. How come you're deigning us with your presence?" She practically sneered the words. Where I was petite with a dark, slanted bob framing my face, Whitney was a tall, willowy blonde.

"It's good to see you too, Whitney. How are things?"

"Never better. You still working for the big ole *Smithsonian*?" Somehow, she pronounced the word "Smithsonian" as if it were a dead, wet rat—a thing to be dreaded and avoided.

"Library of Congress," I corrected her. Her responding laughter was brittle. I ignored it. "What about you? Did you end up becoming a lawyer?"

"Working on it." I noticed she pulled herself up, trying to look taller. "I'm in town for a bit from Annapolis, helping my Granny with some things before we can get a new health aide set up. I heard about your sister."

16

"What about my sister?"

She noted my look and waved a hand at me. "I heard how Rory's finally back on the market now that your sister tossed him out."

"That's not what happened." No matter what happened between Azalea and Rory, I wouldn't have Whitney gossiping so boldly. If she could say something like that to my face, I could only imagine what she'd say behind my back.

"Well, whatever the case, I heard he's available for the first time in about twenty years."

"You planning on asking him out?" I asked.

"I'm not a starry-eyed teen anymore, Juniper. Besides, I have a boyfriend. Georgie works at the Naval Academy." Whitney shook her head and laughed. As much as I had hated Nana Z forcing me to be a third wheel on Rory and Azalea's dates as teens, Whitney had often been a fourth, never able to unglue her eyes from him. Teens with crushes have rarely been the most subtle of beings.

"I've met Rory. He's a nice guy," Tess said. I had forgotten how everyone knew everyone in a smaller town like Rose Mallow.

Whitney made a face like she'd sucked on a lemon. "You know him, do you?"

"We're friends," she said with a shy smile.

"Friends? But he's in his thirties. How old are you?"

"Why?" Tess asked, looking bewildered.

"You're just a kid. He should be with a real woman."

"Whitney!" I cried.

She shook her head. "No way a married man with a kid is just friends with a teen like her."

"It's not like that," Tess said with a pleading voice. "Besides, I'm not a teen. I'm an adult."

"Barely," Whitney replied. She crossed her arms and pointed a strong stare at us, as if daring us to defy her.

"I…. I think you should leave," Tess said. I was proud of her for standing up for herself. Whitney glared.

"She's right, Whitney. You can't harass staff and customers," I added.

"Harass?" She laughed a dark laugh. "You two?" She shook her head. "You know what? I'm not hungry anymore anyway." With a twirl, she waltzed out of the coffee shop.

"Are you okay?" I asked Tess.

She nodded. "Yeah, I'll be fine. That was just weird."

"Yeah, it was."

"Uhm, are you going to order anything?"

"Oh, sorry. I'll take the Chessie Salad but with extra goat cheese and hold the olives, your darkest coffee, a bag of the homemade doggie biscuits, and whatever the Super Spectacular Scone is."

Tess laughed. "Oh, my aunt Harmony bakes those. You'll love it. Trust me. And the doggie biscuits are good enough for people if you ask me."

I didn't know Harmony very well. She had come to Nana Z's funeral – the last time I was in Rose Mallow. Harmony was like a hippie out of time, with her embroidered peasant shirts and headbands around her halo of frizzy red hair. After the funeral, she gave me a cool-looking crystal and promised to smudge some white sage for Nana Z. Or maybe it was light incense. I didn't remember the details well. However, the crystal still sat in my D.C. townhouse near my bedroom window.

I took my order to a table outside and dove into the decadently delicious Super Spectacular Scone first. Salad be darned. The coffee was also amazing, with notes of chocolate and cherries. I hadn't realized how hungry I was.

As I refueled, I gazed around. The view of the Chesapeake Bay was extraordinary. There were lots of full tables. Some people I recognized, although I didn't know most of them well enough to say hello. I noticed one man at the far end of the patio who didn't fit in with the funky, flowing feel of the place. He wore an all-black suit with a matching black tie. It wasn't even loosened. Only a small orange, green, and white pocket square gave any color. He sat ramrod straight, his face was long, and he stared east while clutching a mug of coffee. I wondered what his story was. As a librarian, I loved reading and creating stories, especially about strangers. I decided he was a mafia hit man on the run, hiding out in a small southern Maryland town.

A handsome man biked up to the coffee shop. After he removed his helmet, I couldn't help noticing his dark hair with a lightning streak. He ordered a cup of coffee and a parfait. He sat on a bench next to a bright red bike. For his make-believe story, I determined he was a French billionaire seeking a slice of "real America," which is how he came to be in Rose Mallow. I giggled a bit to myself at these silly notions and polished off my coffee.

As I watched the other customers, Tess left the counter and reappeared in the cafe with a guitar. People clapped wildly. "I'm getting off my shift, so if you don't mind, I thought I'd do an impromptu session." The small audience hooted and hollered in support.

Tess sang a couple of cover songs while she played her acoustic guitar. Her voice was rich and with a maturity that belied her young age. She took famous pop songs and gave them a slower, more sultry sound. I could have listened to her all night.

She gave her special treatment to the Counting Crows' 1990s hit "Mr. Jones," changing the upbeat track to one that was soulful and embraced the song's sad lyrics. Her guitar stripped the melody down to its bare bones. Her voice soared as she described being ignored and unable to believe in herself. I was entranced listening to her version of the song, feeling like she was singing directly to me.

I gazed around the room to see if the song had a similar effect on others. I noticed my so-called "French billionaire" in the corner. He never took his eyes off her. Even from a distance, I could see the pain in them, as he must have connected deeply with her take on the hit song.

After "Mr. Jones" finished, the coffee shop was silent for several moments. It was an eerie shared experience as we all slowly exhaled the breaths we had been unaware we'd been holding. Within seconds, though, the place erupted. People were on their feet, clapping and whistling in support. Tess gave a little curtsy and stepped off the stage for what she promised would be a quick break.

I took advantage of the opportunity to refill my coffee mug. The self-serve coffee station was in the back of the shop, near a hallway leading to the restrooms and kitchen. As I filled up my cup, I couldn't help overhearing Tess talking to someone, but I couldn't see who.

"Can't you see how they're all responding? I know I'm good. I've never been confident like this about, well, anything, but I know I was gifted with this talent. And even if I'm not good, if I'm deluding myself, all I know is that singing is what I was born to do," Tess said.

The sudden sound of grinding coffee beans made it impossible to hear the response. The noise stopped just in time for me to hear Tess reply, "It's my dream. You can't stop me. I've found a way to make it happen without you."

She stomped by me, obviously angry and with tears streaming from her face. As she headed to the stage, people cheered, but the cheers turned to confusion as Tess instead packed up her guitar and abruptly left the shop.

I spotted the "French billionaire" following her out, calling her name and trying to catch her attention. Part of me wanted to follow them, to make sure that Tess was okay, but I didn't know her. As much as I wanted to help, it would be weird. It's curious how listening to a near stranger touch you with a song makes you feel indelibly connected to them, all the while knowing that connection is nothing but a one-way street.

Rory had asked me to meet him at Tidewater Cemetery at midnight when we spoke earlier in the day. I had tried asking him why there and then, but he had refused to explain, just saying "Look, I can't say more yet. There's a lot going on. I know I should've contacted you earlier, but you hadn't been down here in so long, and with everything happening between me and Azalea.... It's a lot, and I wasn't sure you'd believe me. But I need your expert opinion. You're the only book expert that I trust."

"How do you know what any of this is?" I asked. While there were likely history buffs working for car dealerships, I knew he wasn't one of them.

Rory huffed. "I know things. I looked up some stuff."

"Fine, but the O'Doyle diary and its map were created hundreds of years after the covers went missing from Kells Abbey. In Ireland. How did they come to Maryland?"

"I can show everything to you. Believe me, it's the real deal. But it has to be tonight."

I had been torn. I wanted to believe him, but he'd never expressed an interest in books before. Or Celtic history. I hadn't known he knew that the *Book of Kells* existed. I couldn't imagine how he had gotten this O'Doyle diary.

Still, the remote possibility that this was real had tugged at me. Looking at the poorly taken photos of a nearly 400-year-old diary page on a phone screen was less than ideal. No matter what I did, it remained a blurry pic of faded handwriting. I needed to see the original. Then, at least, I could tell if this was an historic document and not, say, an obvious fake made to look that way.

After leaving the Purple Oyster, I walked the boardwalk for a long time, watching the water and arguing internally with myself over whether to go or not. Eventually, I gave in to my curiosity.

It was just before midnight when I pulled up to Tidewater Cemetery. Being there brought back strange but enjoyable memories. As morbid as it might sound, the cemetery had been a popular place for us pseudo-goth teens twenty years ago. Although the gate was locked at night, there had been a sizable hole in the fence line. To my amazement, the hole still existed.

I'd never seen anyone patrolling the cemetery, so it was a great, wide space with plenty of places for teens to hide and make out. My first kiss was here at Tidewater with Tommy Dawson. He gave me flowers stolen from someone's grave. I should have been appalled, but as a sixteen-year-old, I had thought it was such a bold move.

I followed the directions in Rory's texts, which took me to the grave of someone named Tárlach ó Dubhghaill, who had died around 1682, if I was reading the worn stone correctly. I used my phone's flashlight to see if I could get any more details. I took a few photos, although I was uncertain if anything would be legible. On the ground were the brown remnants of a bouquet.

I tried calling and texting Rory's but didn't get any response. I wandered the cemetery and whisper-called his name. I waited for a while, but even at night, it was humid and unpleasant. I watched the fireflies and stared up at the craters on the moon. There wasn't much light pollution out here, so I admired the thousands of stars in the charcoal-black sky. Ten minutes passed. Then thirty. More than once, I spotted a falling star rocketing across the sky. As beautiful as it was, I was also getting eaten alive by no-see-ums. Finally, an hour went by. There was no sign of him anywhere.

More than anything, I was angry. I believed that I was hoodwinked into coming here. After everything Azalea told me, I should have known he was pranking me. Maybe it was worse. Maybe this was some elaborate scheme to mess with my sister.

I threw my hands up in the air and headed to my car. However, with it being so dark, I fell over a footstone and landed in the grass. I hoped I hadn't twisted anything. I pulled myself up to my knees when I saw something behind a nearby gravestone. A shape that seemed awfully familiar.

"Rory?" My voice trembled.

When I stood up, I saw it wasn't Rory. The body belonged to Tess, the spirited barista from the Purple Oyster.

Chapter Three

Tess's body lay across the beds of two graves. It looked like it had knocked over a vase with browning pale roses. I recognized her dyed hair immediately. She was still wearing the same outfit as in the coffee shop except for the apron. I kneeled and checked for a pulse, although I knew the angle of her head was unnatural. I tried shaking her, but she didn't respond. She was dead.

I'd seen dead bodies before. I'd gone on behind-the-scenes tours of the National Museum of Natural History and seen their bones and mummies. Some remains had been unlike anything I'd seen before. There was a mummified person from Peru who was affixed in a permanent seated position. Another person had been turned nearly into soap after being in the water for an extended time. There was a hallway filled floor to ceiling with drawers containing one doctor's collection of human bones.

I thought seeing all of that had meant I had a robust constitution. But finding Tess proved me horrifically wrong. I stumbled a few meters away and threw up behind a gravestone. I collected myself as much as I could manage. I found a cement bench to sit on and plopped myself there.

I tried calling Rory's cell phone again, but he still didn't answer. I texted and yelled out into the empty cemetery, but not surprisingly, no one responded.

As much as I hated doing so, I had two calls I needed to make. The first was to 911. The second was to Azalea.

Within a few minutes, a squad car pulled up, and two deputies climbed out. Their flashlights appeared and disappeared behind different gravestones. I stood up and waved my arms, calling out to them. The male deputy saw me.

He shined a flashlight on me and suddenly came running.

"Azalea? What's going on? Why are you here?"

"Wait, no," I said, putting my hands up.

He ran up to me with his arms outstretched, apparently ready to embrace me, but when he came near, he froze in mid-step. "Who are you?"

"Juniper. Juniper Blume. Azalea's sister."

"Oh, wow, Azalea had mentioned a sister, but I didn't expect you two to look so alike."

"I'm two years younger, but yeah, we've been called twins more than once."

"Torres?" The female deputy caught up to him. She shone a flashlight towards both of us.

Are you the one who made the call?"

I nodded. "Over there." I gestured in the general direction of Tess. The woman wandered over and soon found her. I felt like I'd stumbled into a *CSI*-style television show. I watched her checking on Tess and calling it in. Somehow, my heart sank deeper.

Deputy Torres repeated a question to me. I turned and cried. In between sobs, I choked out a few answers. I kept apologizing. "I'm sorry. I'm so sorry."

"What were you doing here?" he asked for what I think was the third time.

I forced myself to stop crying and explained as best as I could. When I mentioned Rory, I swear I saw him stiffen, but it was hard to say for certain. "I don't understand. You thought he would show you some really old book cover here? In the cemetery?"

I shook my head. "I don't know. He wanted to show me a diary. And a map. They were going to lead him to, well, a treasure, basically. If someone found the missing covers of the *Book of Kells*, why, that'd be priceless."

"And why you? In the middle of the night?" He sounded as incredulous as I felt.

I dropped my head into my hands. "I don't know. I mean, I'm a librarian with the Library of Congress. And his sister-in-law. Soon-to-be former sister-in-law. But he didn't explain why he was going to show me any of this here. In a cemetery. At night." The more I spoke, the more ridiculous I felt. What had I been thinking? The promise of the covers had been a siren song that silenced the more rational parts of my brain.

"Did he say anything about the woman?"

"Tess. Tess…. I don't know her last name. Her aunt Harmony owns the Purple Oyster. She works, well, worked there," I said. Deputy Torres took notes. I had a feeling I'd be retelling this a few more times. "But no, he didn't mention anything about her. I'm sorry, I don't know more."

As I tried to explain, I saw more vehicles pull up. An ambulance and some police cars. Maybe from the county? That would make sense. I didn't imagine that Rose Mallow would have the resources to handle a murder scene. It's such a tiny town. I wasn't sure if the deputies worked for the town or the county.

Then another car pulled up. A dark blue minivan. Oh, no. Azalea. I suddenly regretted calling her. She ran over to us, but the female deputy caught up with her first and held her back.

"That's Azalea," I said, my voice getting weak. Deputy Torres looked over at her. I swear he almost abandoned me to go over to her, but after an extended pause, he turned back and shook his head.

"Do you know where Rory is now?" he asked.

"No. I called and texted his phone and yelled out for him all over the cemetery. I was here for an hour. Nothing. I have no idea where he is."

He asked a few more questions and then confirmed my contact information. "Thank you. Stay in town." He walked away.

"Wait!" He turned back to me. "Do you think Rory is okay?"

He shrugged. "I'm not sure."

My eyes grew wide. "Oh no. Do you think…. I mean, he couldn't possibly?" I stopped myself before saying more.

"What?" Deputy Torres asked.

I whispered the words. "Dead. He's not dead, right?"

"I have no idea, Miss."

My phone buzzed again. I looked down at it. Azalea had texted me. She wanted to know what was happening. "I don't know" was all I could think to write.

"Is Rory okay?"

I did not know. But I knew my sister. If she was hurting before, she must have been reeling now. Even quietly strong people can break. I needed to text something useful. "I'm sure he is. He wasn't here. He'll turn up soon."

The texts.

"Deputy Torres! Deputy Torres!"

I jumped up and ran through the cemetery. Never a smart idea. Once again, I tripped, although this time over a broken headstone. My phone flew from my hand and smashed into a nearby stone before landing in a murky puddle. Fantastic.

Deputy Torres dashed towards me. "What? Are you okay?"

"A bit banged up, but I'm okay." I stood up and tested my legs. Nothing sprained or broken, as far as I could tell. "I was going to send you the texts Rory had sent me."

"What texts?"

"He sent me a picture of the map and a page from the diary. But…" I waved towards the puddle where my phone lay waiting. "Maybe it's backed up." I wasn't sure if my texts backed up anywhere or not. All I could do was hope. And that there would be a cellphone service store somewhere around Rose Mallow. One thing I could say for D.C. was that there was every service or shop you ever needed—and many you didn't—within a metro ride at the most. That wasn't quite the same story down here in rural southern Maryland.

Eventually, I caught up to Azalea. However, before I could comfort her, another car pulled up. I thought it might be more police or a detective, but it was Harmony. How did she hear? I looked at Azalea.

"When you told me it was Tess, I called Harm. I had to."

"Of course."

Harmony flew out of her car and headed straight towards us. "Where is she? Where's my niece?" She carried something in her hand. The female deputy yelled at her to stay back. Harmony froze. "I need to see her. To see my sweet little girl."

When the deputy wouldn't let her come closer, she instead joined our circle of sorrow. The item in her hand was a bundle of what smelled like sage, with several crystals wrapped around it. We welcomed her with open arms.

"I'm so sorry," I said.

"It's the curse," she whispered.

"Curse?" I exchanged a glance with Azalea, but she shook her head, apparently also unaware of what Harmony meant.

"Our family has been cursed for generations. It took Tess's mom—my sister. Also took our father. I smudge and smudge and smudge, but it doesn't seem to be enough."

"What are you talking about?" I asked.

Harmony ignored our questions. She walked around in a large circle, looking up at the sky and then down at the cemetery ground. I could hear her muttering something, but I couldn't tell what she was saying.

"Azalea, child, I'm sorry. I know Rory's your husband, but he's behind this. I can just feel it." With that, she broke off from us and walked away.

I looked at Azalea, who stood there, stunned. Then she crumpled to the ground and wailed. I covered her with my body and held her for as long as she needed.

Eventually, I convinced Azalea to let me drive her home in my car. Deputy Torres promised to drop off her minivan later that morning.

Chapter Four

The morning came far too quickly. In the end, I think I got maybe two or three hours of sleep. Maybe it was because of the lack of sleep that I became resolute in my decision to fix this for Azalea. I was going to find out what had happened. Maybe I couldn't find out who killed Tess, but I could learn more about those documents Rory claimed to have. One way or another, I was going to learn if the missing covers were truly here, or if it was all just an elaborate hoax and what Harmony had meant about whatever Rory had done to Tess.

I caught a glimpse of myself in the tiny bathroom. My face looked like it'd aged a few years overnight. I half expected my short dark hair to have turned white.

I threw on a pair of ballet flats and a simple sundress, tucked some doggie treats in the dress's pockets, and took Clover into the garden to give him a quick break. I promised him a longer walk later, but he didn't seem to mind, as he became invested in an Eastern Tiger Swallowtail butterfly that was exploring the aptly named butterfly weed. He then noticed the gigantic pool of water beyond us and pulled hard on the leash, wanting to take a swim in the Chesapeake Bay.

"Whoa, Clove, not this time. Later, though, I promise."

He cocked his head to the side and looked up at me, seemingly uncertain if I would keep my word. I gave him a few pats and dug out a Purple Oyster doggie biscuit from my pocket for him to enjoy. As he munched on his treat, I knew I had been forgiven.

Afterwards, I walked into the main house to find Azalea cleaning. She had a microfiber cloth in one hand and some unidentified liquid bubbling inside a spray bottle in the other, but she was just going back and forth over the same spot again and again with an absent expression. Clover ran to her feet, helping by chewing at the obviously evil rug. I wondered if Violet was still asleep or not. I came over and took the cloth from Azalea to clean more widely. She shook her head and looked at me, cocking her head to the side as Clover had done minutes before.

"How are you?" I asked.

She didn't answer at first. She stared at me.

"What? Do I have something on my face? My dress?" I turned around and ran my hands down my dress, hoping to smooth down any remaining wrinkles.

"What were you doing there? At the cemetery?"

That wasn't a question I could answer without some caffeine. I put the cloth down and headed towards the kitchen. Clover bounded ahead of me, obviously hopeful someone was getting him food. Azalea also followed, asking, "Why aren't you saying anything?"

"Coffee," was all I replied. Azalea jumped up in front of me.

"Don't blow me off."

"I'm not. But I need coffee." I tried pushing her aside as gently as I could manage. She wasn't having any of that. She pushed me back. Clover growled and nipped at both of our feet. I threw my hands up in surrender. I didn't want to fight with her. "Let's at least sit down to talk."

Her face remained locked with anger, but she nodded slightly. I led us both to the kitchen table but took a detour when I spied the coffee pot on a nearby counter. Thank goodness the coffee pot had worked its magic. I poured two cups. I felt a strange sense of déjà vu, remembering pouring the tea last night.

"Okay, so what were you doing there? What happened?"

"It's where he wanted to meet," I said. Clover resumed playing games with our feet.

"At Tidewater Cemetery? At midnight?" She sounded incredulous.

"I know, I know." I felt like such an idiot. After everything Azalea had said last night, I knew she was right. "I let my curiosity get the better of me. I wanted this to be right. To be real."

"I'm still angry with you," Azalea said quietly.

"I'm angry with myself. I'm sorry, Azalea. Everything you've said. It's all true." I hung my head to my chest. "I missed you. I missed Violet. But coming here was too hard. At least, at first. Then, after it stopped being too hard, I was ashamed for how long I'd been away and that kept me away longer. This adventure felt like an opening to finally return."

"You didn't even call."

"I didn't know what to say. I was a coward," I said.

Azalea rubbed the temple behind her eyebrows with her middle finger. "Yeah, yeah, you were. But I'm glad you're here now. I thought I had lost you."

I leaned over and clasped her in a hug. "Never again. I promise."

She held her hand out with just her left pinky up, like we used to do as kids. "Swear?"

I took her left pinky with mine and nodded. "I swear."

She sighed and rested her chin on her left hand. "Do you.... Do you think Rory's okay?"

I took both of her hands in mine. "He wasn't there, so I'm sure he's fine."

"I just have so many questions. Where was he? Why was Tess there? Who hurt her?" She let go of my hands to rub her temples. "Rory's been acting so strangely. What'd he get himself involved with?"

I tried smiling reassuringly. She didn't need me to echo her concerns. "The police will find him. My guess is that he fell asleep before midnight. He probably wasn't there. Honestly, he might still be asleep now. It's pretty early."

I heard movement on the floors above us. We both checked the clock on the wall. I was wrong. It wasn't that early anymore.

"I should get back to cleaning. The television crew's up already. I shouldn't stop yet," Azalea said suddenly. She poured the rest of her coffee into the sink drain and put the mug in the dishwasher. Before she headed back, Keisha appeared in the doorway carrying a covered casserole of some sort. Clover piped up to see her and the potential of food. He danced around her legs.

"Here. From my mom. A mix of various vegetables and probably some soups. I don't know what exactly," Keisha said, holding the casserole out as if it were a baby with a dirty diaper. I rushed over to take it and found room in the fridge for it.

"Thank you, Keisha, but you're here really early for your shift," Azalea said.

"I know, but I heard about what happened, and I wanted to help," she replied. Azalea wrapped her in a big hug. Although she was only seventeen, Keisha was very tall and towered over my petite sister. Her colorful locs descended around them. "Oh, is that fresh coffee?"

"Help yourself," Azalea said. She headed back into the hallway to continue work.

Keisha poured herself a cup of coffee and added a few generous helpings of creamer. "Honestly," she said to me with a lower voice and a conspiratorial gleam, "The casserole was for my cousin's baby shower tomorrow, but the place will be overflowing with food, so I convinced Mom to give this one to Azalea."

"That was kind of you," I said. She joined me at the table. "How are you doing with it all? Did you know Tess?"

Keisha sighed. "Yeah. She's my older sister Desiree's roommate. Well, she was…" She paused. She looked like she wanted to say something more but wasn't sure how to.

"What happened?" I asked as gently as I could.

"Well, see, that's the thing. They were roommates until a few weeks ago. Tess gave sudden notice about leaving, but she didn't really give any details. My sister was upset because she thought they were best friends. I mean, she hadn't moved out yet, but she had packed her things." Keisha took a sip of the coffee.

That was strange, but it could be for many reasons. "I assume you know Rory?"

"Well, yeah, of course, I know him." She cocked her head towards the hallway Azalea had walked down.

"I mean, yes, of course. What about your sister? Did Tess say anything to

31

her about him?"

"It's a small town. Everyone knows everyone here. But I don't know anything more." She looked around and then leaned in across the table. In a whisper, she asked, "Where do you think he is?"

"I don't know," I said.

"I walked along the boardwalk to come here. There were people talking about it."

"About the murder?" I asked. I knew this was a small town, but I didn't realize that everyone already knew about what had happened overnight.

"Here's the thing, they think he did it," Keisha said.

"He? You mean Rory? They think Rory killed Tess?"

"Well, yeah. People think Rory killed Tess and ran off. That he's hiding," she replied.

"But why would he do that?" I remembered what Harmony said in her rambling about moving a curse onto Rory. I still didn't know why she felt he was involved, but I figured that was the source of the gossip.

"I don't know. Do you think he could do that?" she asked.

"No," I said, although my voice was firmer than I felt. After what Azalea told me about the so-called trinkets, I didn't know what to believe. I'd known Rory for nearly twenty years, but I'd never have thought him capable of such meanness. Maybe I didn't know him well after all.

"I don't know. Azalea won't tell me much, but I know he's hurt her. I mean, not in the same way as what happened with Tess, but...." She stopped, apparently realizing she was tripping over her own words. She took a breath. "Look, people are already talking. I think they just want to know where he is. Running away makes him look guilty."

"You think he ran away?"

"You think he didn't?"

Fair enough. I knew nothing more than anyone else at this point. Before yesterday, I never would have dreamed Rory capable of hurting anyone, let alone a seemingly sweet young woman like Tess, but as I thought about it, I really wasn't sure anymore. I hoped the police found Rory soon.

"I'm going to poke around online later and see what I can turn up," Keisha said.

"I'm sorry—what?"

"Oh, nothing major. Just going to pour through social media and look through a few feeds."

I didn't like the sound of that. "I think it'd be better if you stayed out of it. Let the police do their job."

"I won't do anything dangerous. I want to help Azalea find out what happened. Rory might be her ex, but he's still Violet's dad, and they've at least been polite together in front of me. That's more than I can say about my own parents when they had marriage problems." Keisha rolled her eyes and shook her head. She went over and refilled her coffee mug.

"Okay," I said. "Let me know if you find anything. Can you do that?"

"Of course," she replied.

I ran into the Chronos Channel crew packing up in the Wildflower's lobby. There were four people checking what I presumed were camera, light, and sound equipment. Maybe other things, too. I avoided Ms. Collins and the goateed man and headed instead towards a young woman with bouncy curls. She sported a tattoo that looked straight out of the children's book *Dinotopia*. Now, that was someone I was interested in.

"What's going on?" I asked her.

"Prepping for Bradford's big announcement," she replied as she futzed with a camera case. Then she looked up and said, "Oh, hey, aren't you the chick who found the dead barista girl last night?"

Well, that was one way to put it.

"Yeah, unfortunately."

"I'm so sorry." She sounded genuinely concerned. "What were you doing out there?"

I shrugged, uncertain of how much to tell her or anyone. Obviously, word was getting around quickly. Rose Mallow was a small town, sure, but this all happened just last night, and these were hotel guests, not townsfolk hanging out at the local watering hole. Maybe I should put it out there and try to control what people were imagining on their own.

"I don't think you'd believe me if I told you."

"Oh yeah?" She motioned over to one of her colleagues, an older man who was probably at least six-foot-six, if not taller. He towered over us. "Try us."

"Have you ever heard of the *Book of Kells?*"

The woman's eyes went wide. She looked at the man and then back at me a few times in a near-comical fashion. "Wait, wait, did you go through our stuff?"

"Your stuff? No, why would I do that?"

I was perplexed. Meanwhile, the goateed man joined our trio. Ms. Collins pretended we didn't exist, but she stayed within earshot. The group all started talking at once, largely ignoring me.

"Out of everything you could have said."

"She's just messing with us."

"But what if this has something to do with what he's planning?"

"Has anyone actually seen the book?"

"Okay, everyone, stop," said Ms. Collins from her spot at the registration desk. She strolled over to us. "Let's try this one at a time, shall we?" Her attitude reminded me of my first-grade teacher, Mrs. Cloister. She pointedly turned towards me. "Miss Blume, why don't you explain further about what you mean and what took place last night at the cemetery?"

I tried to summarize as best as I could. As I did, I saw the group exchange glances. Some checked their notes. When I finished, Miss Collins nodded. "Well, that's interesting, isn't it? Uncanny, really."

"It seems like everyone here knows something that I don't," I said.

Miss Collins nodded. "Yes, it certainly does. But we can fix that for you. You should join us at Bradford's announcement. I think you'll find it... illuminating." With that, she walked back away to go back to whatever it was she was working on.

"If Ruth says you should come, then you're welcome to join us," said the woman with the *Dinotopia* tattoo. "Happening around 11 a.m. at the Calverton Golf Course. If you can get there by 10:30, that'd be ideal."

"Isn't he promoting his book? Why is he talking at a golf course?"

She shrugged. "I don't know all the details. He's staying with Leonard Calverton at their family estate, though. So maybe that's why. All I know is that he was adamant about being there."

Interesting. I had long heard about the Calverton family, one of the oldest in Maryland. I also knew they ran a big bank and owned much of the land in the area and. Every now and then, one of them became a local politician or small-time celebrity, but more than anything, I knew they were incredibly rich, unlike most of the town. Even as just a summer visitor, I was well aware that everyone in Rose Mallow knew of the Calvertons. They were more mysterious than anything else, rarely, if ever, commingling with the commoners. I sometimes saw them at one of Nana Z's charity benefits, but that was about it. I mainly remembered some old, white-haired people in outfits that probably cost more than my annual salary.

Before going to the announcement, though, I needed to get my phone fixed to get the photos from the texts. Finding an actual carrier retailer was a good forty-minute drive out of the way. I knew I'd never make it there and back in time. I'd need to find some other way to find the images off my phone. Keisha was back at the front desk. Perfect.

"Okay, you're my digital sleuth, right?" I asked her. Keisha grinned at my description. "I broke my phone during my misadventure last night. Rory had texted me two images, and I'm trying to figure out how to get to them."

She thought about it. "Have you tried logging into your service provider's account? Or do you know if things get backed up to the cloud?"

I wasn't sure, but it was worth trying. We took turns on the inn's laptop, trying to figure it out. After about fifteen minutes and a few wrong turns, we found them. I couldn't resist hugging her. Keisha sharpened the images as best as she could and then printed them out as large as possible on the inn's printer.

Even adjusted and enlarged, the images remained hard to see and read. I laid them out on the registration table and used an inn notepad to take notes. Keisha took one look at them and shook her head, unable to provide any additional help.

"You've already gone above and beyond," I said. She beamed at me and watched as I tried to unravel the pages' mysteries. However, one of the Chronos Channel team needed something, so she went back to helping them as they readied for the press conference.

"Okay, Rory, where'd you get these from? What do they say?" I said to myself. I started with the map. It had the word "Mallow," but there was a different word in front of it. I wasn't positive about what that one said. Could this be somewhere else entirely? I thought of the inn's library. Maybe there was a history of the area here. That seemed like something Nana Z would have had. I darted over and skimmed the books. No luck. I'd have to tell Azalea to get one. Or maybe I could find a copy to give her.

"Hey Keisha, can I borrow the laptop? I want to see if there are old histories of the town that have been digitized," I asked when she finished with the television crew. She handed it over to me. I searched as best as I could, but I only found snippets of things, nothing comprehensive. I gave the laptop back to her and wondered the best next steps to take.

"Is the historical society's office open?" I asked.

She searched online. "Yes, but it's open for limited hours, basically whenever they have volunteers to staff it. Looks like they might be open this afternoon."

Okay, so I wouldn't make it there before the announcement. But maybe I could get there afterwards. It was certainly worth trying, at least.

Next, I focused on the page from the O'Doyle diary. Parts of the sheet were so faded that I couldn't read anything. Of what was legible, some words appeared to be in Irish, or maybe they were encoded. If they'd been in Hebrew, I would have at least been able to put some of my Bat Mitzvah training to use, but unfortunately, that wasn't any help here. I spent the next thirty minutes piecing together what I could. When I finished, this is what I had put together:

> *Saving K- from Crom.... priority.... Dublin is not.... Maryland provides.... welcomes Catholics.... ó Dubh....*

It wasn't much, but at least it was something. My spidey research sense was definitely tingling, but I wasn't yet sure what all it meant.

"Didn't you want to get to that announcement thing by 10:30?" Keisha asked.

"Yes."

"You better get going. You're going to be late."

Chapter Five

I hit the road with KG and sped over to the Calverton Golf Course. Along the way, I caught sight of a few faded signs for the old Baytastic Amusement Park & Zoo. Pretty sure that place shut down the summer after we graduated high school. Nowadays, I cringed, remembering the wild animals in tiny cages with thick bars and concrete floors. So far removed from the more modern work at recreating a more natural environment for them. Even so, I had fond memories of going there each summer. We'd ride the rickety wooden roller coaster, play carnival games, and eat way too much funnel cake.

Baytastic was where Azalea and Rory went on their first date together back in high school. Soon, it became their favorite place to go. I was ordered to tag along. I don't know if Nana Z thought I would be a chaperone or if she had something else in mind, but mainly, I was a third wheel, usually unable to find my own date. Besides, they always ditched me as soon as Nana Z was out of sight, so I ended up wandering the place on my own for a few hours at a time. As fun as it was, being there alone multiple times got boring quickly, especially when I didn't have any extra cash.

I blamed Azalea at the time, but looking back, I knew she was just young and in love. She wanted to move to Rose Mallow as soon as she graduated high school to be with Rory. However, our parents and Nana Z ordered her to go to college first. I think they were trying to break the two up, but it didn't work. She and Rory got married all of three weeks after she graduated. She started working at an antique store, while he found handyman jobs before working for a car dealership.

I wanted to go anywhere else besides Rose Mallow. Sure, I had made a couple of decent friends here, but I wanted to see the rest of the world. Driving around now, though, I hadn't realized how much I had missed this place. I wondered how many of those old friends were still local. Maybe I should look them up after everything settles down?

Although I got to the press report a little late, the television crew was still setting up. Although there were a few media folks there, most people were milling around. I think many looked confused why they had been sent down here to the middle of nowhere. It didn't look as formal as I had expected. I had imagined a stage and backdrop with chairs in neat rows for a dozen media outlets. This looked more like an impromptu cocktail party with a few video cameras around.

"I know you." Orson Bradford, the titular Professor Treasure Hunter, strolled up to me. "Who are you with? CNN? NBC? One of those web things?"

"I'm not press. I'm a librarian."

"Librarian. That makes sense. With Smithsonian?" He looked like he was still trying to put my face together with his memory. After he drunkenly hit on me at the last Society of Rare Book Librarians conference, I wasn't particularly interested in helping him figure my identity out.

"No, Library of Congress."

"Aha! The good ole LOC! I'm glad they sent you. They should be excited about this finding. It is extraordinary." His smile was enormous, and his teeth were almost neon white. They positively glowed. He sported a neatly trimmed white beard that matched his close-cut white hair. He wore rimless rectangular glasses. He reminded me of a Santa Claus in a J. Peterman catalog.

Should I explain? Would it help or hinder? I couldn't decide.

"They didn't send me."

However, I don't think he heard. Instead, a look of recognition splashed across his face. "Oh goodness…. Library of Congress…. Oh no. You were the young woman at the SRBL conference. Your name was, I mean is, something floral. Lily? Daisy?"

"Juniper."

"Right, right. Juniper." To my surprise and amazement, he bowed low in front of me. "My dear Juniper, I must apologize. After my talk at the conference, well, I hadn't eaten enough, but I had too much to drink. If my rather fuzzy memory serves me correctly, I was rather uncouth towards you that evening. My deepest apologies for my behavior."

I was impressed. He had seemed so full of himself at the conference that I would never have imagined him capable of an apology. I hadn't expected him to remember who I was, assuming I was just another face in the crowd for a celebrity like him.

"May I make it up to you?" he asked. "Would you be kind enough to join me for lunch at the Calverton Club? I'd love to introduce you to my dear friend Leonard Calverton. As a librarian, you'd appreciate their family's collection of colonial-era materials."

This was hard. As much as I didn't really want to spend time with him, the opportunity to see the family's collection was intriguing. Perhaps they had something that might shine light on this whole *Kells* mystery.

"Yes, I'd love to—"

Before I could finish my sentence, Ruth Collins popped in. "It's time to start, Orson."

Orson bowed again. He took my hand and kissed it. I wasn't crazy about the gesture, but I appreciated the sentiment. Ruth certainly didn't. She hunched her shoulders and made a face. Her top lip squeezed into an unhappy Elvis Presley curl. I wasn't sure if that was directed at him or me.

I settled into the crowd. I spotted Deputy Torres from last night, alongside a woman I hadn't seen before. She was tall with raven black hair pulled into a crisp bun. Her face suggested she was from India or of Indian descent. She sported an all-black pantsuit with a deep orange blouse and an expensive set of sunglasses crowning her head. I wondered both about who she was and about Deputy Torres. He obviously knew Azalea, but I was picking up some vibes I couldn't quite name.

Before I could think about it further, Orson Bradford walked up to the lectern and started talking. "Today is a momentous day. For more than a thousand years, a treasure of the world has been missing without a trace.

Now, centuries later, we finally have substantial clues to hopefully lead us back to this masterwork."

He paused and took a sip of water from a cup on the lectern. "Yes, ladies and gentlemen, the rumors you've heard are true. Today, we begin the journey of rediscovering the missing covers for the *Book of Kells*. Here in Maryland."

Hands immediately flew up around me, but I wanted to fall down. How was this possible? How did he know about the *Book of Kells* connection to Rose Mallow? He must have spoken to Rory, but when and how? The coded language of the television crew this morning suddenly made more sense to me. They knew this was coming. I looked over at Deputy Torres and the woman beside him. Did they know? Is that why they were here?

Orson fluttered his hands in front of him to shush the crowd. He continued, saying, "There will be time for questions shortly."

He gave a rough history of the *Book of Kells*. Ruth placed a very large photo of one of the illustrated pages on an easel behind him. He explained about the mysterious covers, which may have been a physical shrine for the book more than just a hardback covering, and how all is known is that they were golden and bejeweled.

"But how could the *Book of Kells* be in Maryland?" asked a reporter, interrupting Orson's history lesson. I thought she was from ABC, but I wasn't positive. "Here in, uh, Rose Mallow?" She consulted her notes to check the town's name. "Isn't that book in Ireland?"

"The book is indeed in Ireland," said Orson, staring down his nose. "But I'm talking about their covers. They were removed and disappeared long ago."

"What makes you think they're here? Do you have any evidence?" another reporter asked.

"Yes, yes, yes. Of course. Ms. Collins?" He gestured towards her. She pulled out another large image. A familiar one. It was the map that Rory had texted me. Still faded, but not nearly as much as mine had been. I suspected their team had better Photoshop skills than Keisha or I did.

"A treasure map, if you will, to the location. You see this X here? That is where we are now, at the Calverton Golf Course. And I am pleased to announce that the Calverton Family, under Leonard Calverton himself, has granted permission for us to conduct an archaeological survey of this area. Good news, it won't impact anyone wishing to play a round," he said. There was some polite laughter, but mostly, I saw confused faces, ready to interrupt with more questions.

I had several questions myself. I had a strong feeling that he, too, knew about the diary, since the map wasn't much without that context. Mainly, I wanted to know how he had acquired them, since as of yesterday, they had been in the hands of my currently missing brother-in-law.

Orson took a few questions, but he gave vague answers. He promised little when it came to a timeline, except to say they'd invite everyone back "soon."

When asked about why Maryland, he went on a lengthy discourse, saying in part, "As we all remember from our school days, Maryland differed from the other colonies. We of course, remember the Puritans in New England and the Quakers in Pennsylvania, but Maryland wasn't the Protestant utopia some of these other places were. Instead, this colony was founded as a Catholic safe haven. When Oliver Cromwell was leading his own version of a holy war across the British Isles, hundreds, if not thousands, of Catholic believers descended on Maryland for safety and the freedom to practice their religion.

"It was during this time in the 1650s that we believe a group of Roman Catholic refugees from Ireland escaped to Maryland. They brought their holiest of treasures, one they had been secretly safeguarding for centuries, here to escape persecution. The covers of the *Book of Kells*."

There was a sudden silence as everyone considered what he said. It lasted mere moments before there was a flurry of activity. People rushed up to him, wanting to know more. He waved them away and hurried out under the watchful eye of Ruth Collins.

After the announcement, I debated who to follow. I didn't really take Orson seriously about the lunch offer, and besides, he had been whisked away pretty quickly. There was the mysterious woman with Deputy Torres that had piqued my interest, but I assumed that if the police wanted to speak with me, they knew how to find me. The rest of the TV team was still packing up, so I went towards them. Perhaps they could elaborate more about his remarkable announcement.

I found the woman with the *Dinotopia* tattoo. "I'm sorry, I still don't know everyone's names," I said. She laughed brightly and held out a hand.

"Ashley Mullers." She pointed to the rest of the team as they worked on packing up. The tall man was Eric, while the goateed guy was Jeremy.

"Does Ruth work for the Chronos Channel?"

"Oh, uh, sort of. She's Orson's personal assistant. We're more of a roving crew working on various assignments," Ashley explained.

"That was a very unexpected announcement," I said.

Ashley nodded. "Yeah, I guess more for you than most others. How weird is it that you came to town for the same reason?"

"How weird indeed." The woman with Deputy Torres walked up to us. She held out her badge. "Detective Lakshmi Gupta. I'm investigating the death of Tess O'Doyle and the disappearance of Rory Walsh. I take it you're Juniper Blume?"

I nodded. Well, at least that explained who she was. Looking at her badge, I saw she was with the county's sheriff's office.

"Have you found anything more yet? Have you located Rory?" She gave a quick shake of the head but didn't elaborate. "Okay. So then, what can I do for you, Detective?"

Meanwhile, Ashley took this as a cue to back away. She focused on packing, but she was still obviously within earshot range. I wondered if this would all end up on TV somehow. I shuddered at the idea.

"I wanted to talk to you, since we didn't cross paths last night," Detective Gupta said.

"Right now?" I looked around, noting the various media outlets still cleaning up. I really didn't want to talk more around them any more than I did around the Chronos Channel folks.

"Not here. Why don't we connect a bit later today so you can give me your version of events?" The detective handed me a business card.

"My cellphone was broken last night, but I will call you from the Wildflower Inn," I said. "But I accessed the photos from my phone. Did Deputy Torres tell you about those? I'll email them to you once I'm back."

"That'd be good. I'll also be having a little chat with the *Professor* over there to learn a bit more about his documents," Detective Gupta said.

I couldn't help asking, "Don't you think it's strange?" She cocked her left eyebrow. "I mean, that Rory told me about this 17th-century diary with a map and that Orson has one, too? Do you think it's the same one? Maybe one's a fake? Or maybe they both are?" I was thinking aloud as I talked. The detective listened intently. "I think it's a remarkable coincidence."

"I don't believe in coincidences."

"I don't either." There had to be a connection. I didn't know what it could be. At least not yet. Was Orson somehow involved with Tess's murder and Rory's disappearance? However, I had a hard time imagining that he would flaunt the diary if he was. Perhaps I had underestimated his ego. I didn't like it, but I knew I needed to have his promised lunch date. Maybe that would reveal more.

Then, I remembered something the detective said. "Did you say that Tess's last name is O'Doyle?"

"Yes," she replied.

"That's what Rory called the diary. He said it was the O'Doyle diary."

"Interesting," she said, but nothing else.

I promised the detective again that I'd check in with her soon. In the meantime, I headed towards the club and hoped that I could finagle my way in to see Orson. It seemed like half of the press junket had the same plan, as we were all trudging across the golf course to the club's dining room. Multiple large, bulky men stood guard at the door. They refused to let anyone in without proper ID or a guest.

"But Orson promised that we'd meet for lunch," I said to the men.

"Sure, sure, Miss. And my wife promised me a fire truck for my birthday," replied the one on the left. He was bald with a single gold earring.

The man on the right perked up at this. "I hope you get it."

The left bodyguard sighed and shook his head. "Ignore him. Either way, you're not getting in."

"Oh, and why not?" Orson came to the dining room door. "Juniper, here, is my most interesting date. Did you know that this fantastic woman works for the Library of Congress?" He held his arm out, which I reluctantly took.

"I didn't," said the guard on the right with the amazement of a small child. "That's the place with every book ever published, right?"

"Not quite every book," I explained, but Orson shook his head and swiftly ushered me inside. The bodyguards didn't stop him. As soon as we were past them, I dropped his arm.

"I'm so pleased you'll join me. It'll be much less noisy—and nosy—in here." Orson walked quickly with broad steps. I had to double-time to keep up with him. He led me to a foursquare table at a window overlooking the golf course. "Here, here, please."

I sat down and debated what would be a "sensible" lunch to get. Probably salad. That seemed to be the acceptable and professional option. Not that it's what I wanted. While I've had a few decent salads in my life, the majority have involved bland lettuce soaked in a monsoon of dressing. Would I have to pay for this? I was scared to look at the prices on the menu.

"Get anything you'd like. My treat. Personally, may I suggest the steak?"

"Thank you. I'm a vegetarian, but I appreciate the recommendation."

"Then may I steer you towards the absolute best pasta you will ever taste, short of going to Italy, of course? They make it from scratch in-house and use this delicious array of wild mushrooms. It's perfectly doused in a truly decadent cashew cream sauce. Oh, I may decide to get it myself," Orson said. His eyes got a dreamy look, apparently recalling the last time he had enjoyed the dish. It did sound magical, but that much pasta also sounded like it'd put me down for a long afternoon nap.

"Now, Orson, is a heavy, rich pasta the best choice for a TV star?" Ruth appeared from nowhere. She began to take a seat, but Orson flashed her such an incredulous look that she stopped in midair, creating a very awkward version of yoga's chair pose.

"I believe that this decision is between my guest and myself." Each word was a dagger thrust directly at her. I was shocked by how cold he suddenly became. "Besides, I have asked Juniper here to discuss an amazing, certainly life-changing opportunity."

"I don't have any of these details," Ruth interjected. She apparently wasn't going to give up without a fight.

"You wouldn't. Now, may I have some privacy? Why don't you join the TV crew for a bit?" He waved her away with a flick of his wrist. I watched a parade of emotions quickly pass across Ruth's face, including what was obviously outrage and disgust. Each feeling disappeared almost as soon as they had started, and she put on a stoic, neutral expression like a mask. With that dismissal, she nodded, almost bowed, and then moved on.

I was unsure of how to respond after that unsettling incident. What had transpired between them? Was he going to suddenly turn cold to me? I was shocked when he turned back to me, all sunshine and smiles.

"My apologies for that interruption. Now, my dear Juniper, I saw your presentation at the Society for Rare Book Librarians conference, and it really stuck with me. You are obviously smart as a whip. Although I've never known why that was the saying? Anyway, may I ask you what you know about the *Book of Kells*?"

I was taken aback. I probably should have expected the question after this morning's announcement, but for whatever reason, I simply hadn't. I wondered if he knew about my connection to the O'Doyle diary and Rory and how much to say.

"I know it's one of the most incredible books ever created. Seeing *Kells* in person in Dublin was one of the biggest highlights of my career. That the missing covers would be here in Maryland, of all places. Why, it's almost beyond my imagination."

"Ah, but as you say, it's 'almost' beyond." He leaned across the table towards me. "I need your research expertise. Here is what I know. Maryland was a place Catholics sought refuge while Oliver Cromwell and his army trampled through Ireland in the mid-1600s. So why wouldn't some Irish believer bring them here, far away from his reach?"

"Fair enough," I said, "except the covers had already been missing for over 600 years by that point—long before the first colonists landed anywhere in North America. Besides, before long, this so-called Catholic safe haven became quite the tough place for Catholics to live. Have you heard of the Toleration Act?"

He shook his head. After Rory contacted me yesterday, I spent much of the afternoon catching back up on my Maryland colonial history to better understand if it made sense to bring the covers here. I found some of it to be surprising.

"The Toleration Act was created in 1649 to help ensure religious freedom between Catholics and Protestants," I told him. "However, the Act didn't develop as some great proactive measure. Instead, it was passed in response to rising tensions. So, would this have been a safe place to bring the covers, assuming they still existed? I'm just not sure it adds up."

"Interestingly, the only person ever to be prosecuted under the Toleration Act was Maryland's first known Jewish resident, a Portuguese immigrant named Jacob Lumbrozo. Down in St. Mary's City, he was tried for blasphemy. As much as the Toleration Act had been billed as supporting religious tolerance, no one apparently considered that there might be any other religions here as well." Being Jewish, I couldn't help shaking my head.

To my surprise, Orson chuckled. "I like your inquisitive spirit, Juniper."

He might have said more, but the waiter appeared to take our order. I threw caution to the wind and got the mushroom pasta Orson had suggested. After we ate, Orson turned to me and said, "I have a proposal for you. I need a researcher of your caliber. Would you consider joining me on my quests?"

I sat there dumbfounded for a few moments. Instead of answering him directly, I asked what had been bothering me since this morning began. "How did you learn about the covers being here? How did you know about the O'Doyle diary?"

Orson nodded. He must have expected the question. "I received a, well, let's say it was a 'communique,' if you will, from a person in the area. At the moment, I'd rather not name my source, but I have had people authenticate it. It was good enough for Leonard Calverton to fund this exploration of ours."

"Have you seen the covers yet? I've heard they might not be traditional book covers but more of a shrine that had enclosed the book." I pictured a golden reliquary covered in filigree and encrusted with gemstones, but I didn't know if that was accurate.

Orson hummed. "Well, no, not yet, but…." He leaned across the table towards me. "That's why it will make for such good TV to be there when they're unearthed. To get that raw emotion." He paused for a moment, apparently considering his next words. "Besides, the person giving me the diary can't back out now if the entire world is in on it."

"Wait." His words struck me deeply. "Giving? Back out? You don't have the diary yet?"

"I have enough to get started. Several nice scans were sent to us. I was supposed to have more, but I think my source got cold feet." He shrugged, but I caught a dark look slide across his face.

I sat there, confused. "But what about Rory disappearing?"

This time, confusion crossed over Orson's face. "Who is Rory? Oh, wait, is that the man the police are searching for? Something to do with that bartender's death?"

"Barista," I corrected automatically. "And…." I was about to say that, of course, these things were connected, but I realized he didn't know. Either he was a better actor than I had ever given him credit for, or he honestly did not know that his pursuit was connected somehow to last night's events. Not that I yet knew how they were connected, but it seemed impossible to me they weren't. Who was his source? What had the person promised? And was that person part of why Rory was missing?

Before I could say more, a good-looking young man interrupted us. He had a movie star feel to him. He sported an immaculate suit with thin pinstripes that honestly could have been pure spun silver. There was a streak of pure platinum through his dark hair, although his face suggested he was barely older than thirty. "Please excuse me, Orson," he said, "But I wanted to check to see how things were going."

"Oh, fine, fine. Leonard, may I introduce Juniper Blume? She is a rising star at the Library of Congress, although I'm hoping she can be convinced to join my team," he replied.

Leonard? This was Leonard Calverton? I had expected a much older patriarch, perhaps even older than Orson. Looking closer at him, I decided Leonard had to be around the same age that I was. There was something familiar about him, but I couldn't place where I had seen him before.

Leonard flashed a truly brilliant smile. "An absolute pleasure, Ms. Blume. Please, though, call me Leo. You're from the Library of Congress?"

"Yes, although I'm not representing them. I'm just here because I'm curious about whether the *Kells'* covers are really in Rose Mallow." I decided not to mention anything about Rory and Tess.

"Perhaps I could give you a tour?"

"You need to agree, Juniper. Their collection is a real treat." Orson said with what I believed was a genuine smile.

"I'd love to join you." I was incredibly curious to see the collection. Besides, I wasn't sure how to respond to Orson's proposal, so getting away would give me time to think through his offer.

Leo and I walked down a long hallway with large windows facing the club. He led me to an elevator and took it down a few levels to where the collections were stored. "It's grown to quite the collection, really. My grandfather started it—mainly focused on documents and objects important to colonial Maryland. My mother expanded the focus to early America. And now, I'm working on ensuring everything will be properly cared for and can be shared with anyone interested. My family has been resistant to opening our treasures to the public, but I don't see how it helps anyone if it's cloistered away here."

"Yes, that resonates with me. Working at the Library of Congress is an honor, but we exist to serve everyone—regardless of who they are or where they come from. I believe deeply in sharing information as widely as possible." I thought back to an argument I'd had with my boss, Greyson, yesterday morning. He was great at collections stewardship but terrible with the general public, typically acting like the Library of Congress shouldn't be for everyone but only those who met his snobbish standards. He didn't seem to think I met them either. I paused, remembering our argument. Was that yesterday? It felt nearly a lifetime ago.

"I'm glad you feel that way. I wish everyone did. My family has long been viewed as 'kings on the hill,' but I truly want to change that perception." He fiddled with his keys to find the right one to open the first collections storage area. He paused and ran his hand through his hair. Then I remembered where I'd seen him before.

"Do you ever go into town?" I asked. He looked like the so-called "French billionaire" that I had seen in the Purple Oyster yesterday. If it hadn't been Leo, it must have been a close relative. It was unnerving to realize that the billionaire part might be right. Even more unsettling was realizing he would have been one of the last people to see Tess alive.

"From time to time, but honestly, I felt unwelcome there, even having grown up in the area. I feel like everyone is always staring at me." He shrugged. He found the right key and opened the door wide for both of us to go through.

"You should try visiting Rose Mallow again," I said lightly.

He considered it and said, "Well, I might if you would join me? Perhaps for dinner? Tomorrow night or the night after?"

Before I could agree, I caught sight of the storage room in front of me and gasped. It was the size of a floor at Ikea. Although I'd worked at the Library of Congress, I wasn't numb to the absolute pleasure of being beside so many documents and materials that helped tell the story of America's creation. It took everything I had not to run and dance through the aisles. I glanced at Leo, unable to form words, but hoping that my entire being beamed my excitement. He laughed and nodded. I didn't need more assurance but took off to explore the storage space, a literal warehouse of history.

There was a rack with paintings and prints by John Singleton Copley, William Peale, and other notable early American artists. I spotted an 18th-century powder horn carved by John Bush, one of the earliest known African American artists. There were document boxes filled with letters, diaries, and other written materials from an array of early American people: founding fathers and mothers; abolitionists and enslaved people; loyalists and patriots; visitors from other countries; and so many more. An entire section was dedicated to the native peoples whose lives were turned upside down by the colonists.

I don't think I saw more than a small percentage of what the family had collected over the generations. To see how this reflected what a rich and remarkable collection they must have felt like an understatement. I felt I could spend years here before I got to know everything they had preserved.

"You might find this section interesting," said Leo, leading me over to an area dedicated entirely to Maryland history. He pointed out a cabinet focused solely on Rose Mallow. My whole body tingled with excitement.

I perused the file folders inside. There wasn't much from the earliest years in the 1600s, but I noticed a preponderance of old Irish surnames: ó Dubhghaill, ó Súilleabháin, Breathnach, among others. My hand found my mouth. Was it indeed possible? Could one of these families have brought the *Kells'* covers here? I wanted to go through everything, but there wasn't time now. I wished I had my phone to take photos. My quick examination yielded nothing obvious about the *Kells*, but it was possible I had missed a good deal.

"You never answered my question," Leo said. I looked up, not remembering what that question was as I had become so engrossed in the files. He laughed. "Dinner?"

I shook my head. He immediately looked crestfallen. "Oh, no, I didn't mean no. I just meant what an idiot I was for forgetting. I was so overcome by this remarkable collection. It's beyond incredible."

"So, is that a yes or a no?"

Before I could answer, a young man and woman appeared in the room, laughing loudly and carrying what looked like a large bottle of wine with them. The man looked like a younger version of Leo, so I assumed this must have been his brother. I wondered if I had been wrong, and if he had been the man who had followed Tess. I wished I had paid more attention.

They looked more dressed for a nightclub than the golf club. He sported a shiny black shirt with a gold dragon over the left shoulder. The shirt had a few buttons open, exposing way too much of his smooth chest. Her dress was bright red, extremely low cut, and clung to her every curve while glittering with sequins.

Given the woman's smeared make-up, I wondered if they had just come home from a very long night out. I didn't know of any nightclubs near Rose Mallow, so I suspected they had driven quite a distance.

"Leo! Leo! Leo!" the young man chanted his name and raised the bottle up high. Upon closer inspection, I could see that it wasn't wine but Dom Perignon champagne. I knew little about champagne, but I suspected this wasn't the cheap stuff I picked up at the local wine store to make mimosas.

"Leo, Leo, Leo," the woman copied him, although her words were far more slurred and with an accent I couldn't place. She hung onto his other arm with about as much conviction as the tight dress nearly falling off her shoulders.

"Cecil. Why are you down here?" Leo's voice took on a tinge of anger, but he kept his face stoic and straight.

Cecil nodded his head towards me. "Same as you, looks like. Somewhere secret to get away from good old Daddy's prying eyes."

"This is Juniper Blume. She's a librarian from the Library of Congress." I spotted tints of red poking up along his neck. I noticed he gripped his hands tight.

"Seriously, Leo? A librarian. I mean, excuse me," he said, briefly turning towards me with an abrupt nod, "But come on. You finally come back home after all this time away, and you still can't live a little? I mean, at least she's cute."

"Excuse me?" I spoke up.

"Leave her alone. She's not some...." He stopped before describing Cecil's date with a word he'd obviously regret.

"Oh, Elsa here? How are you doing, sweetheart?" Cecil asked her. She gave a weary thumbs up. "No offense, uh, Junie...."

"Juniper," I said.

"Right, right. Whatever. Anyway, Leo, you've been gone awhile. You can't just come back and have a whole big hurrah over this *Kells* thing and expect everyone in the family to suddenly jump in line." Cecil punctuated his thoughts with the champagne bottle.

"That's not what I'm trying to do," Leo replied.

"Hey, more power to you, you know? If I had failed as spectacularly as you did in Italy, I'd probably have rushed home with my tail between my legs, too. I mean, sure, I respect that you're trying to cover up that disaster with this far-fetched scavenger hunt."

"I want to go on a scavenger hunt," said Elsa. Her accent struck me as Scandinavian, but I wasn't positive.

"Hang tight, honey. We'll play a few games in a bit," replied Cecil. I felt gross listening to him, but Elsa just giggled.

"Get out." Leo nearly whispered the words.

"I'm not going anywhere. I'm going to go on a scavenger hunt or two with the stunning Elsa here. Did you know she's the daughter of the Swedish ambassador?" He laughed and sauntered toward his date.

"Cecil. Get out. Now." Leo's voice was considerably stronger this time.

Cecil stopped in his steps. Elsa turned with a wide-eyed expression. "CeCe, maybe we could go back to my place?"

Cecil locked eyes with Leo. Neither spoke, but they stared deep at each other for a long time. I felt awkward witnessing this. Elsa looked entranced. Her gaze darted between the two of them as if she were at Wimbledon.

Just as I almost broke in, Cecil beat me to the punch and said, "All right, all right. Honey, we'll find somewhere else to play our 'reindeer games.'" I shuddered at his smarmy style and felt instantly relieved when the two strolled back out of the storage room.

"I'm so sorry about that," said Leo with a shake of his head.

"It's not your fault. I mean, unless, did you want to talk about it?"

Leo looked at me like I had spoken an unknown language. I wanted to shrink down. Then he dropped his head towards his chest. "No, it's okay. My brother may be a creep, but unfortunately, he's right. All of this..." He waved his arms around the room. "And the hunt for *Kells* is a chance to start anew. Cecil has a head for business, but unfortunately, that's not my specialty. My passion is history. Maybe he's right. Maybe this is a stunt."

"What happened in Italy?" I asked. I still wanted to find out if he was the man I'd seen go after Tess at the Purple Oyster, but I had a feeling I'd be kicked out of the site and given a restraining order if I tried right now.

He shook his head. "Sometimes research projects don't always pan out."

"What were you researching?" I asked.

"I led an expedition to find the lost hoard of King Alaric," he replied.

I shook my head. I knew a lot about history, but I didn't recognize the name at all. "King who?"

"In the early 400s, Alaric of the Goths sacked Rome. He then held the city hostage until the Roman senate coughed up over 5,000 pounds of gold and 30,000 pounds of silver. Hundreds of millions of dollars' worth today. They still looted the city for three days. Then Alaric and his thugs headed south with their treasure, terrorizing the region," Leo explained.

"Oh wow. I hadn't heard about any of this."

"I'm not surprised. Most people haven't, even though it's this immense treasure that disappeared."

"What happened to it?" I asked.

"Alaric died before he could cross into North Africa. Supposedly, the treasure was buried with him under the Busento River in southern Italy, and everyone who knew the location was murdered."

"That's messed up."

"Yeah, it really is. And it's been missing for centuries," he said.

"So you thought you'd find it?" I asked.

He shrugged. "I tried. I failed."

"That's quite the concise synopsis."

Leo laughed. "Yeah, well, it's an understatement. I invested a lot of money, brought a lot of so-called experts with me, and spent about three years on the venture. We found absolutely nothing." He opened and closed his right hand like a magician to illustrate his point.

"So why are you trying again with the *Book of Kells*?" I hoped I didn't sound snarky asking, but I couldn't believe that after such a spectacular failure, someone could turn right back around and try again so quickly and easily. I wasn't sure if that was a sign of resilience or being stubborn.

Leo nodded. "I mentioned that this collection was created by my grandfather, right? Can I show you something?"

He walked the aisles until he found a nondescript gray box on a shelf. He pulled it out and carried it over to a table. I watched as he opened it, flipped through various folders, and picked out a few photographs. He spread them out across the table. The photos were all in black and white, although based on the material of the photographs and the clothing people wore in them, they seemed to come from different time periods.

"My family made its fortune in several ways. Railroad barons, bank owners, shipping magnates. If there was a new way to make money, my ancestors loved to try it out. Sometimes they failed, but they succeeded often enough," Leo said.

"So your family has developed some strong stomachs for failure."

"You could say that. And they didn't just love exploring new business opportunities. They also loved exploring. This is a photo of my great-great-grandfather and grandmother following a paleontological dig in Montana." He pointed to the oldest image. It was a carte-de-visite, mounted on a card featuring two people in a photographer's studio holding up a large, fossilized femur. I suspected it was from a dinosaur or maybe a wooly mammoth.

"Here's my great-grandparents on an early expedition to Japan." This couple sat in front of a pagoda-style temple with an enormous mountain behind them.

"And here's my grandfather." He held up a smaller black-and-white photograph of a man in a military uniform. "Have you ever heard of the Monuments Men?"

"The program that sent curators and historians into World War II to save priceless art from being stolen by the Nazis?" I asked.

"Yes, that's the one. He was part of that effort. Helped recover the Ghent Altarpiece from a salt mine in Austria." As he spoke about his ancestors, I noted the pride in his voice.

"All of this is because of their efforts." Leo spread his arms out wide.

"Incredible. So you wanted to follow in their footsteps and lead an expedition yourself?"

"Basically, yes. I don't have the head for business that my siblings have. And they don't have my love for history and culture. They constantly start new businesses, and most implode. No one blinks an eye because, eventually, one takes off. I wish they'd have the same understanding for my search for history's missing treasures," Leo said.

Everything he said made sense to me. Like me, he was obviously deeply influenced by his grandparents and had inherited their love of history and adventure. Unlike me, he had significant resources at his fingertips that could try to solve some of these cultural mysteries. I was feeling a little jealous of that distinction. I also felt bad that his efforts had not yet succeeded and were obviously not appreciated, at least not by his brother Cecil.

"I was going to say yes, you know."

He looked surprised. "To dinner?"

"Yes. If that's still an option?" Truth be told, my motives were only partially pure. I thought he was attractive, but just as much, I was curious about Leo Calverton. Was he the one who ran after Tess? Was all of this a stunt to impress his family? What else existed in these archives?

"Great," Leo replied, looking relieved. "What do you think of going to the Indigo Room? It's been a long time since I've been there, but I remember it being very nice."

"Sounds good."

"Very nice" sounded like it was a swanky place with an expensive menu. I didn't think anything like that had existed in Rose Mallow. Had the Indigo Room existed when I was last here? If it had been here when I was a teen, I'm sure I would have considered it too fancy. Now I hoped I had a dress nice enough to wear.

As I finished up with Leo's tour and headed back to the golf club, I glanced across through the hallway windows and spotted Orson outside arguing with the other man I had seen yesterday in the Purple Oyster—the one I had imagined was with the mafia. As with before, he wore another well-cut suit, although from the distance, I couldn't tell if it was navy or gray today.

Although I couldn't hear them, the action between them was dramatic. Orson waved his arms, obviously unhappy with the man. Oddly enough, the gentleman looked almost relaxed. He stood beside an iron table and occasionally stopped to sip on something in a teacup. I guessed it was coffee or tea. Orson became so enraged at this that he knocked the cup from the man's hand. Again, he seemed to take it in stride, simply leaning over to pick it up. Orson apparently gave up after this and stomped away.

The man sat back down at the table and signaled to a waiter to refill his teacup. Before drinking again, he paused and looked directly at me. Our eyes locked, and I felt as if he recognized me, although I didn't know who he was. Goose pimples spread across my arms. I pulled away from his gaze and speed walked away as fast as I could politely manage.

Chapter Six

When I returned to the Wildflower Inn in the late afternoon, Azalea was a ball of semi-controlled rage. She gripped the railing of the stairs so hard that I was almost afraid a decorative curl would come off in her hand.

"Where have you been?" Her voice had that even-toned grit that Nana Z's used to get when she was holding back anger. "It's been hours since the announcement ended, and I hadn't seen or heard anything from you. It's almost five o'clock now, and you left after ten in the morning!"

"I'm sorry." I tried to explain about lunch, the tour, and remind her about my phone, but she threw her hands up in the air as her anger exploded. She bounded down the stairs and got up into my face. Although my older sister was a couple inches shorter than me, it didn't feel that way as she berated me.

"Rory is still missing. You were missing for hours. What were you thinking? What if you had truly gone missing, too? How could you do this to me?" Her voice rose to a crescendo. My heart sank. I hadn't realized how much my willingness to go with the flow of opportunities today had impacted her. I knew this came from a place of love, but I felt lower than low to have scared her so badly. I wrapped my arms around her. She pushed away, but then instead, simply sank into my embrace.

"I can't have you gone too, Juniper."

After a long moment, we let go. She said, "There's something I've been wanting to show you."

I followed her back through the house and out into the garden. We passed the beds of blue hydrangeas to the Carriage House, where I had spent the night on the floor. I felt bad about her seeing all my stuff littered about the floor, but then again, the place was overflowing with dusty boxes. She walked through the box towers until she found one and pulled it out, placing it on an open spot on the floor.

"What's in here?" I asked.

"Look." She opened the box for me to peer inside of. I saw stacks and stacks of what appeared to be leather-bound journals. With great care, I pulled one off the top and opened it up to the first page.

My mouth dropped open when I recognized the signature scrolling across the first page. "Are these Nana Z's watercolor journals?" Azalea nodded. The hard-bound book was filled with thick, textured white pages with deckle edging. Nana Z had filled the pages with her vibrant paintings of Rose Mallow. I recognized her loose style, where she essentially sketched with her paintbrush. She loved vivid colors. There were pages devoted entirely to painting her beautiful Queen Anne style house and lush gardens, overflowing with native Maryland flowers. She initialed each page and marked it with the date. This book was from over twenty years ago. I was amazed at how similar her work looked to the gardens and view still. It made me both miss Nana Z while feeling proud of how Azalea had maintained her vision.

"Thank you for sharing these with me," I said as tears formed in my eyes. I closed the journal and held it close to my heart.

"Looking through them makes me feel like she's still here," said Azalea.

"Oh, she is, she definitely is. She's everywhere in this house and gardens. We should get some of these paintings framed."

Azalea nodded. "I thought that too. We have a few of Nana Z's watercolors already up, but I'd love the Wildflower Inn to become a tribute to her."

"You could create a gallery in the library."

"Keisha suggested we put some images on the website and social media too."

"That's a great idea."

Before we could brainstorm further, Azalea got a text message from Keisha about a need in the house. "Why don't I let you poke through these more, and we'll catch up over dinner?"

"That would be great."

I spent the next hour sifting through the journals and reconnecting with our grandmother's artwork. I found several devoted to her travels around the world. As much as I wished I had inherited her artistic talent, I at least had received her love for travel. I missed going to different countries, meeting new people, and exploring the culture. I just wished I had done some of that with her.

After looking through the journals, I carefully returned them to their box and stood up to stretch. My whole body felt a bit compacted from sitting so long on the floor. I really needed to get back into yoga. There wasn't enough space here, but I tried to stretch out as best as I could manage. Of course, being cramped and clumsy, I knocked over another box.

This box was different from the others. First, it wasn't a cardboard moving box that had been carefully taped shut and labeled with a summary of the contents. It was a simple lidded box, so naturally, the lid flew off as the box fell down, and the contents went flying everywhere.

"Fantastic job, Juniper," I said to myself.

Inside and across the floor were scattered a series of envelopes, letters, and other papers. I didn't mean to look through them, but it was difficult not to as I cleaned up. To my surprise, everything was fairly recent and addressed to Azalea. After looking through Nana Z's old journals, I guess I had expected these to be some of her old papers, too.

Most of them were from Calverton Bank, the same bank run by Leo's family. Apparently, they also held several loans on the Wildflower Inn. I should have realized how expensive it was for Azalea to retrofit the house and turn it into her dream hotel, but I hadn't understood how much everything had cost her until I flipped through the letters.

As I tried to pile back up the papers, I discovered Azalea hadn't kept up on her loans. The letters grew increasingly more urgent, they came more frequently, and the dates became more and more recent.

I wondered why she hadn't told me about any of this. Not that I had this kind of money to help, but maybe I could do something. Had she told anyone about these loans? Had Rory known? I didn't see his name on any of these.

As I put the box back, I worried Azalea might lose the inn.

After cleaning up, I went back into the inn, planning to ask Azalea about the papers. It was well after six in the evening now. However, before I could say anything, Deputy Torres and Detective Gupta entered the inn's foyer. They didn't have any news about Rory, or about Tess' murder. At least nothing that they would share with us. Mainly, Deputy Torres poorly tried hiding his puppy dog eyes for Azalea while Detective Gupta pulled me aside to get my side of the story. I ran through what had happened Friday as well as I could, trying not to leave out any detail.

"So, when you got there, there was no sign of the O'Doyle diary?" Detective Gupta asked me. I steered her into the library, and we sat in matching chairs upholstered with a wine-red damask. A small wooden table stood between us.

"I wasn't really looking for the diary at that point. I couldn't find Rory anywhere." As we talked, Azalea appeared with a full tea service. She didn't bother asking if we wanted anything to drink. I suspected she wanted an excuse to stay in range of our chat. Detective Gupta didn't seem to mind. She poured a cup of Darjeeling tea for both of us. I added sugar and cream, but she drank hers straight black.

"Do you think the diary could have been there while you were waiting for him?" She sipped her steaming hot tea.

I thought for a moment. "Maybe. Probably. Like I said, I didn't really know what to expect at that point."

"Do you have any idea how he got the O'Doyle diary?" she asked.

I shook my head. "Honestly, it doesn't make sense. He's never been interested in history before. Last I heard, he worked for a car dealership."

"He never expressed any interest in the antique shop I used to work for," said Azalea as she poked her head back into the room.

"Ms. Blume-Walsh," the detective said with a note of caution.

"Oops. Sorry, don't mind me," Azalea said with a way-too-cheery smile and a sheepish wave. She disappeared back out of the library.

"Why did he want to meet you in a cemetery? Why at midnight?" Detective Gupta asked.

"That's a question I've been going over again and again in my head. He didn't explain on the phone. All I could think was that he wanted a secretive location, one where we wouldn't be easily seen or overheard. But beyond that? I honestly don't know." I blew across my tea. I felt like I had several pieces to this puzzle, but they weren't fitting together yet in a way that made sense, at least not to me.

There was a lull in the questions while the detective drank her tea. I figured it couldn't hurt to volley one at her. I expected she would probably bat it away, but it seemed worth exploring. "Detective, do you know why Tess was there?"

She sighed. "It's still too early in the investigation to have all the details." So no, she didn't have a clue yet either why the young barista was dead in the cemetery.

"Do you know anything about Tess's family's curse?"

Detective Gupta half spit out her tea. She put her cup down and dabbed at her suit with a cloth napkin from the tea tray. Fortunately, her pantsuit was nearly cobalt black, so it was unlikely anything would show up. Today's blouse was a deep, bright fuchsia. "I'm sorry. Did you say a family curse?"

"Harmony, Tess's aunt, brought it up. She claimed that some strange curse had killed her father, Tess's mom, who was Harmony's sister, and now Tess herself. She didn't elaborate on the details."

"Well, that's…unexpected."

"I'm surprised Harmony didn't mention it," I said.

"We haven't been able to talk with her yet," said the detective.

"Oh?"

"We will soon. As soon as the sedative she took fully wears off." The detective closed her eyes and shook her head.

"Sedative?" I asked. "Is she in the hospital?"

The detective made a face. "No. Apparently, a friend gave her an Ambien to help her rest, and she's still passed out from it."

"So you also don't know yet if the O'Doyle diary is connected to her family?" I asked.

"Not yet, but we'll talk to her soon," she replied.

I wanted to ask more while the detective was at least partially answering me, but Azalea came back into the room, carrying a duster. Clover trailed behind her. When he caught sight of me, he dashed over and bounced into my lap. She hummed softly to herself as she went through and carefully dusted every single book in the library. She wasn't fooling anyone.

"Mrs. Blume-Walsh."

"Oh, please, call me Azalea." Her cheery grin was a bit too forced. Meanwhile, Clover jumped down to pounce on Azalea's shoes. She ignored his playful antics.

"Fine, Azalea. Was there something you wanted to add to the conversation?"

"Oh, me? Just keeping the place clean for everyone. Don't want anyone coming home to an unclean house. Could you imagine the reviews they'd leave?" She chuckled to herself. My sister was many things, but she was definitely not an actress.

"Did you two talk already?" I asked. Clover darted over to the detective and me. The pup went back and forth between us, apparently sizing up who would be the better playmate. Detective Gupta reached down first to pet him. He rewarded her with a million kisses. Not that she seemed to mind.

"Yes, we had a long conversation about my 'relationships' earlier." Azalea put the word into air quotes while holding the duster. Upon hearing Azalea talk, Clover raced back over to his other favorite person.

"Relationships? Plural?"

Azalea rolled her eyes. Detective Gupta said nothing, but she took another sip of her tea. Given the tiny smile playing at her lips, I think she was enjoying the show we were putting on. I wanted to ask Azalea if she meant Deputy Torres, who I assumed was just beyond my line of sight, but I didn't want to ask anything too specific in front of the detective.

Instead, I went on asking, "What else did you discuss?"

"Well, primarily Rory's family history."

"I didn't think he had much of a family history?" From what I remembered, Rory had been raised by some distant aunt who had died years ago. As far as I knew, Azalea and Violet were his whole family. It was fairly one-sided at the wedding, although most of their mutual friends sat on his side so that it wasn't completely empty.

"Yes, he was adopted."

"Not raised by a distant aunt?" I asked.

"No, he was in and out of foster homes for most of his childhood. So, he never really knew his background. I explained that to the detective." Azalea nodded towards her. Then she laughed. "As a holiday present, I'd gotten him one of those genealogy website subscriptions, because he wanted to find out more of his story. He even did a DNA test."

Clover decided it was my turn next. He jumped into my lap and started licking my face. His tongue tickled.

"I did one, too. You'd be shocked to learn that you and I are 99% Ashkenazi Jewish from Eastern Europe." She laughed, and so did I.

This wasn't remotely a surprise. Our parents had met in Hebrew school in Baltimore. Both sides had come to Maryland in the 19th century from Germany and modern-day Poland. Ashkenazi Judaism referred to those of us with ancestral roots in Germany and East Europe, unlike Sephardic Jews who came from the Mediterranean area. I couldn't help but wonder what that final 1% might comprise. With all this talk about Ireland, I really hoped that a surprising part of us had turned out to be Celtic.

"What about Rory? What did his DNA test determine?"

"He turned out to be much more of a mutt. British Isles, Germany, Russia…. All over Europe."

"Did either of you get any matches? Find any long-lost parents or siblings?" As I asked, Clover jumped back down and over to attack Azalea's feet as she moved. Detective Gupta listened to everything we said with silent patience. I don't know if she found our conversation remotely interesting or was humoring us to see if she could glean more useful information.

Azalea shook her head. "Nothing closer than a fifth cousin each at the time. Unless he got a match more recently that he didn't mention to me. With the separation, it hasn't exactly been a big topic of conversation for us lately."

"Well, at least you know for sure you're not related to each other." It was a joke, but Azalea frowned at me. I peeked over again at the detective, who listened intently with that Mona Lisa smile. I wondered what she suspected so far. Given her stoicism, I figured that I'd not want to go up against her in a poker game. Well, not that I could recall the last time I had played poker.

"Oh, no. Clover!" Azalea cried out. My young dog had an accident on the library's antique rug. Detective Gupta and I both jumped up to help Azalea. The detective took him aside while I ran over to the front desk to get Keisha's help. She found the rug cleaner, gloves, and paper towels. Soon, we had the mess as cleaned up as it was going to get for the time being.

After that, the detective and I chatted for a little longer, but I don't think the rest of our conversation was fruitful for either of us. I led her back into the inn's foyer, where we met back up with Deputy Torres. As I had suspected, he had been waiting just outside the library and undoubtedly listening intently.

"Will you keep us updated?" I asked her.

"I'll do what I can," the detective replied.

"Good to see you again, Azalea," said Deputy Torres.

Azalea nodded with a shy smile. "Yeah."

The two of them reminded me of her and Rory as teenagers. Part of me thought it was cute, another part wanted to puke, and a third found it very creepy, given Rory being missing.

"Just wish it was under better circumstances," I said.

Torres turned to give me a look as if I smelled like I hadn't showered in days. It took everything I had not to make a face back at him. Azalea didn't seem to notice. She had gone back into the library to take a second try at cleaning up after Clover's mess. My dog's mess.

"I better go help her," I said. The detective nodded and headed to the door. Torres lingered, looking longingly at Azalea, until Gupta tugged on his sleeve and gave him a pointed look. He nodded sheepishly and followed her out.

After they left, I played with Violet for a while. I gently roughhoused with her and Clover in the gardens behind the inn. We played a version of hide and seek around the flowers, except that neither of them really understood how to play. It was beyond adorable. Violet would get stomping mad if she wasn't the one to tell me where to hide. "Over here!" She'd point to a bench and have me sit on it. Clover jumped up on my lap and licked my face. Violet covered her eyes and counted to three. Then come find me. When we traded places, she wanted me to tell her where to hide, as Clover skittered around our feet.

Nana Z would have been proud of how much Azalea had done with her gardens. If the place had been left to me, the half-acre of land would have fizzled and turned brown, as I had not inherited her green thumb. I still grew up appreciating the remarkable display the flowers put on. They grew in a well-orchestrated riot of colors, sizes, and textures, interlaced with gravel pathways. There were rounded rows of beds, filled with Black-Eyed Susan, blue and pink larkspur, several types of lilies, and a dazzling mix of hydrangeas. Below a few older oak trees was a small woodland wonderland with hostas and ferns. The towering trees provided shaded respite from the increasingly scorching summer sun, although at least it was starting to drop. At least with being on the Bay, there was a refreshing breeze coming from across the water to us.

I thought about how the garden would look later in the season when the rose mallow would start. The town was covered in the native hibiscus with its red, pink, or white flowers. I gathered up Violet and Clover, and we headed inside for something to eat.

In the kitchen, Azalea was ahead of me, already prepping some apple slices as part of dinner for her little girl. "Thanks for playing with her. It's exciting for her to have her aunt here."

"My pleasure. She's a lot of fun!" I poured a tall glass of water for myself and joined Violet at the kitchen table. "Do you know if the historical society will be open tomorrow? I want to look up a few things about the town's history there. Keisha told me earlier, but I forgot the exact times they're open."

"Not sure, but it's an all-volunteer place, so they don't keep regular hours," Azalea replied.

"Do you want me to bring Violet with me tomorrow? Give you a longer break? She could be my helper." I turned to Violet and said, "You want to be a helper, right?"

"Helper! I can be a helper!"

"We'll see about tomorrow." Azalea looked at the clock and then spoke to Violet. "It's almost seven now. Sorry to rain on your parade, sweetie, but it's past time for your dinner, bath, and then getting ready for bed."

"Ah," I said with a whine, not wanting to give up time with my niece. Azalea shot me a glance that told me to cool it. Fair enough. She had a hard enough time getting a spirited nearly four-year-old to go to bed.

As Azalea took Violet away, I headed outside to give Clover a quick walk around the block. I was getting hungry, so I figured I'd give him dinner, and then maybe I'd head downtown to grab a bite to eat at the Purple Oyster. After all the excitement, I realized I needed a bit of a break.

When I got down to where KG was parked on the street, I discovered that some of my tires were flat. It took me a moment, but I realized they weren't just flat. They had been slashed. To top things off, a message had been sprayed across my windshield, saying, "GO HOME!"

Chapter Seven

Well, that's not smart. How can I go home if the tires are slashed?" A mix of anger and fear jolted through my veins. Why would anyone do this? Why to me?

I ran back into the house. "Everything okay?" Keisha asked from the front desk.

"Unfortunately, no. Do you have a camera back there? Or can I borrow your phone?" Not having a phone was becoming increasingly inconvenient. I'd need to get that fixed shortly.

Keisha handed me her phone. I called the police and explained what had happened. She listened with wide eyes. While I waited for them, she came with me outside, and we took photos of the damage.

"Do you think we should cover it or something?" Keisha asked, looking around the neighborhood. The vandalized car stuck out amidst the perfectly manicured neighborhood of pristine historic houses. I didn't want the Wildflower Inn to stick out in such a negative way.

"Probably. But not until after the police come back. I don't know what they're going to say."

Deputy Torres arrived within a few minutes. He whistled low upon seeing the car. "That wasn't like that when we left earlier." He circled around KG. "And you don't have any idea who would do this?"

"Not a clue. I only got to town yesterday."

"Feels longer than that," he said. I wasn't sure how to interpret his tone, but he didn't seem happy. "I'm going to need to tell Detective Gupta about this."

"You think it's involved with Tess and Rory?"

"You think it's not?" He looked incredulous. He turned to Keisha. "Where's Azalea?"

"Down the hall. Putting Violet down for bed." He continued to stare at her. "Oh, okay. Yeah, why don't I go get her? She'll probably want to know about this." He nodded.

As Keisha headed back into the house, Deputy Torres came up to me. "You've rankled someone pretty hard."

"Yeah, but who? Why?" I tried to balance on the curb. The ground on either side felt like a pool of lava that was ready to melt me. Why would anyone care this much about me?

He chewed on his bottom lip. "Sure is a pretty car. You kept it without trouble in D.C.?"

"Never had an issue before. The neighborhood around my apartment is pretty quiet."

Capitol Hill was a busy place, and although I wouldn't leave any doors unlocked there, I hadn't encountered any issues. My street was tucked away from the main drives and felt more residential than downtown. I had a pleasant mix of neighbors who kept an eye out for each other. I'd never felt unsafe there.

"That must be nice. You must miss your home."

"Well, sure. But even with everything going on, it's been nice to see Azalea again."

He nodded but said nothing at first. Then he said, "You know, you'd think D.C. would be a busier place than Rose Mallow."

"Yeah, it is." I didn't care for his tone. My hands found their way to my hips.

"Normally very quiet around here. We rarely have any trouble." He looked up and down the street pointedly. I followed his gaze. There were a few people working on their gardens and a couple walking dogs, but otherwise, it was the definition of peaceful.

"I'd imagine not." I tried to keep my tone neutral, but I don't think I succeeded.

"Bet you're eager to get back to the city. Probably quieter there than it's been here for the past, oh, I'd say, twenty-four hours or so." He waved his hand to punctuate his comment about time.

"Deputy Torres, is there a point you're trying to make?"

He looked me square in the face and said, "Yes, yes, there is. You waltzed into your sister's life yesterday after being away for a long time. And you brought a whole host of craziness with you."

My mouth gaped. "What are you talking about?" Not that I didn't know how chaotic things had been, but I didn't see how his accusation was fair.

"She was going through a lot before you came back, and now, instead of taking some of that burden off her shoulders, it seems to me you're putting more on." His eyes narrowed as he spoke.

That was a low blow. "Oh."

"You want to help your sister?"

"Well, yeah, of course." I wondered if he was pushing at me because he obviously liked Azalea or because he thought I was interfering with the police's investigation. Not that I had done any investigating, at least not on purpose. But either way, I had obviously struck some sort of nerve with him. And someone else, based on the attack on my car.

"Then I'd suggest you stay out of things. Keep a low profile."

"I'm not in anything," I replied.

"Right. Where were you about to go in your car?"

"To grab some dinner. Tomorrow, I'm heading to the boring old historical society. And to get my phone replaced." I pulled out the broken one."

"And that's it?"

"That's it. See, nothing nefarious. Not stepping on anyone's toes. I promise."

He looked at me with suspicion. "Look, if you find anything in the historical society about all this, I want to be the first to know about it."

"Of course." I held my hands up in mock surrender.

As I brought them down, Azalea came back out. She took in what happened to my car and proceeded to nearly smother me in a giant hug. Deputy Torres hung back, but he watched us intently.

Over the next half hour, I filled out forms while pictures were taken. After Torres finished up, Keisha found a tarp to drape over KG so the neighbors wouldn't stare. He checked in with Azalea and then headed out.

The group of us must have drawn our neighbors' attention anyway, because soon Whitney came out of her grandmother's house and down to us. She made it down before we got the tarp on, so she saw the full extent of the damage. She whistled and asked, "What happened here?"

"I don't know. But I guess I've upset someone," I replied.

"Sure looks that way. What'd you do?"

"I honestly have no clue."

"She did nothing." Azalea stuck up for me. She came around in front of me and stood there in a classic Superman pose. I was touched. "There's some crazy person out there."

Whitney shrugged and looked away. "I don't think people do these kinds of things without a reason."

"What reason could there be to do this?" Azalea asked. I wondered how often she had confrontations with Whitney and her grandmother. That couldn't be fun to do regularly.

"No idea. But it seems to me like you've ticked someone off pretty good," Whitney said as she turned to me. I saw a smile trying to burst across her face, but she appeared to be trying to tamp it down. Always great to have a next-door neighbor frenemy. "Well, good luck with finding out who you made mad. I've got to get going. Need to grab some things from town for Granny. Interviewing a new health aide again tomorrow. Maybe this one will work out."

"You go through a lot of interviews. Even on a Sunday?" I asked.

Whitney shrugged. "Granny doesn't trust all these new people. She keeps wanting me to move down here. But I tell her about my job and Georgie and…. She's too proud to say she doesn't want anyone else to see her like this."

"Not the perfect matriarch of Rose Mallow?" My tone was snippy, and Azalea shot me a look, but to my surprise, Whitney seemed unconcerned.

"Yes, essentially. She's always been about perception, you know?"

71

To my surprise, I felt a pang of sympathy for Whitney and her grandmother. It had been a shock when Nana Z died, but at least it happened suddenly. She was so strong until the very end, and just like that, she was gone. It had been such a surprise, but at least she hadn't suffered. I wondered what I would have done if Nana Z had needed help. Sure, Azalea was already here, but she was also married and pregnant. Would I have given up working at the Library of Congress and returned to Rose Mallow to help? I'd like to think so, but honestly, part of me was glad I hadn't needed to find out.

"Do you want to move back here?" I asked.

Whitney made a face. "I have a life in Annapolis."

"Sure, but—"

"We'll find her an aide." She turned, ending the conversation, and headed back to her grandmother's house. I must have hit on a soft spot. I hoped they figured out what worked best for them.

"I still need to figure out how to get to the historical society tomorrow," I said.

"Oh. You can use my bike," said Keisha.

"That'd be great. Are you sure you won't need it?"

"I'll be fine," Keisha promised.

"Looks like they will open around eleven tomorrow morning," said Azalea. She had looked up the information on her phone.

A phone. Something else I needed to take care of. Hopefully, places would be open on Sunday. I briefly wondered about sending my boss Greyson, and others at the Library of Congress an email through the Wildflower Inn's computer about being delayed a bit, but that could wait until I had more information. I didn't know how long it'd take to repair my car or replace my phone, not to mention that Rory was still missing. I had no idea how much longer I'd be here in Rose Mallow. But I was sure I'd get back before the work week started.

"Hey, it's Saturday night," Keisha said.

"Yeah?" I wasn't sure why that needed an announcement.

"Movie Night. Starts at eight pm." She did a little shoulder dance.

"You remember Movie Night, right? The town does a weekly movie showing in the summer months out at the Redbud Park," Azalea said. I had forgotten that tradition, although it'd always been fun to go to as a teen. Redbud Park was at the south end of the boardwalk, past the Wildflower Inn and other historic homes that backed to the walkway and the Chesapeake Bay. It was named for the many beautiful eastern redbud trees planted there.

"What are they showing tonight?" I asked.

Keisha was already checking on her phone. "Too bad. It looks like it's Hitchcock's *North by Northwest*. Old stuff. I prefer when they show things like *The Karate Kid*."

"I loved that movie when I was a kid," I said.

"What do you mean when you were a kid? Was Jaden Smith even born yet?"

I laughed. "Oh, you mean the remake."

"It's a remake?" She looked genuinely stunned. I sometimes forgot that cultural references were different for teenagers. I suspected that was the case for Nana Z watching Azalea and me.

"Besides, how can you not love *North by Northwest*?" I asked. "Or anything with Cary Grant. He's amazing."

"Yeah, sure," she replied, sounding unconvinced. "Honestly, I don't think I've ever seen anything with him in it."

"Oh, that stings." I pretended an arrow had pierced my heart. "We definitely have to fix that."

"I do like *North by Northwest* a lot, but personally, I prefer *Rear Window*," said Azalea. I couldn't argue with her there. That was also my favorite Hitchcock movie. Even if it didn't have Cary Grant, it had both Jimmy Stewart and Grace Kelly.

"Do you want to go? I can stay here and watch the inn and Violet," Keisha said. "Oh, and take Clover too. The park is dog friendly."

"I'm pretty sure he's curled up with Violet in bed," Azalea replied. I would not break that duo up. "Are you sure, Keisha?"

"You've had a hard day. Watch a movie. Take your mind off of things." Keisha practically pushed us away.

"Okay, okay. Yeah, I think a movie might be good. I'll grab a blanket for us to sit on and meet you in the back garden?" Azalea said to me. She and Keisha headed inside.

I walked away, but that's when I noticed that no one had picked up that day's mail, which stuck partially out of the mailbox. I went to grab it to bring into the house. I probably shouldn't have shuffled through it since it wasn't mine, but I did it without thinking. There were not one, but three notices from Calverton Bank in the mix. I thought about returning the mail back to its box, but Azalea had reappeared on the wraparound porch.

"I meant to ask if you wanted to bring a snack. I mean, there's generally a few vendors or food trucks at Movie Night, but I don't know how good their vegetarian options will be," she said with a smile. Then she noticed what was in my hand. "What do you have there?"

"Bringing in the mail," I said.

"Oh, uh, thanks." She darted down the porch stairs to grab it out of my hands. "I'll drop these inside."

"I saw the loan notices," I said. Azalea paused mid-step, facing away from me. She slowly lowered her lifted foot to the ground. "When I was going through the box with Nana Z's watercolor journals. I accidentally knocked another box over and saw..."

"You read my mail?" she asked, still not facing me.

"I thought they were Nana Z's letters."

"I see." She paused. Neither of us said anything for a long moment, but she broke first. "Well, what's done is done. Not like you seeing them makes them suddenly vanish." She turned back and sat down on the porch step.

Why did I suddenly have a feeling we were going to miss Movie Night? My heart plummeted into my stomach.

"How bad is it?" I asked.

She shrugged. "It's bad. If I don't pull things together, I'll lose the Wildflower Inn. Maybe by the end of the summer."

"Can I help?" I asked.

Azalea gave a dry laugh. "On a librarian's salary?"

"Maybe I can help. Who else knows?"

Azalea sighed. "No one. Not Rory. Not our parents. No one." I opened my mouth to say something, but Azalea cut me off. "And they will not know. I'm going to figure this out."

"You don't have to figure it out alone," I replied.

"Oh, right. What are you going to do? Move down here to help? I'm sorry, Juniper, but I don't think running an inn is exactly your forte. I've seen your cooking and cleaning skills. Unless you know something about marketing and accounting?" Her gaze jabbed deep into the heart of me. I know she wasn't trying to be mean, just realistic, but her assessment of my skills still stung.

"I can look up resources and help. I am good at researching and finding solutions. And I've managed projects, budgets, and people before." I may have felt defensive, but it was all true. Besides, before I worked in libraries, I had done so many odd jobs in between traveling that I felt like I had a pretty good primer at helping with most businesses. However, I reminded myself that this wasn't the time to reinforce my resume. Azalea needed help and sympathy.

"Have at it." She waved her hands, as if washing herself of it all.

I joined her on the porch steps. When she didn't push away, I placed my right arm around her shoulders. "We'll figure this out. I promise. Maybe I can sell my townhouse and rent for a bit instead."

She looked at her feet. "You sold me your half of the inn years ago to pay for that townhouse. I won't ask for that back."

"My townhouse isn't our grandmother's home. It's just a place. But we're getting ahead of ourselves. Maybe it won't come to that," I said.

"Maybe." She didn't sound convinced.

"Look, we won't solve this tonight. Do you still want to go to Movie Night? Take your mind off things for a bit?" I stood up, but my sister remained uncertain.

"You really think we can figure this out? I feel so awful worrying about all this when everything with Rory...." She didn't finish her sentence.

I crouched down beside her. "Yes. We'll figure this out. And Rory would want you to figure it out as well. Whatever happens between the two of you, I know he wouldn't want Violet without this home, right?"

"Yeah, that's true." She sighed.

"Why didn't you tell him?" I asked.

She shrugged. "When things started falling apart between us, I, well, I thought I could do this all on my own. I'm not like you. I've never lived on my own. I didn't build up a career, getting to work at the world-famous Library of Congress. So, I wanted to prove to everyone that I could make this inn work."

"Everyone? Or yourself?"

Azalea nodded. "Both, really. So I don't want anyone else's help in fixing this. I will fix it."

I reached over and hugged her. At first, she stiffened, but then she relaxed into it and hugged me back.

"I'm sorry," said Azalea, "But honestly, with everything, I don't think I'm up for the big town-wide Movie Night."

"No worries. I have a different idea," I said. Azalea looked at me with a mix of uncertainty and hope. "We'll do Movie Night here. That way, Keisha can come too."

Azalea nodded. She followed me into the house, and we found Keisha to explain.

"Are you sure?" she asked.

"Definitely sure. Where do you guys want to watch a movie?"

"Let's go into the library," said Keisha, pointing to the same room where the detective had interviewed me earlier in the afternoon. "There's a good-sized TV in there, and I can still keep an ear out for the front door if needed. I'll put up a sign. We should get one of those bells you ding for service."

"Yeah, we can do that. But you know what we need first?" Azalea asked. Her voice suggested she was warming up to the idea.

"What?" Keisha asked.

"Popcorn. Lots and lots of popcorn. I'll get started on that if you two pick a movie. We don't have many DVDs that aren't for three-year-olds, but we can stream something."

"Did you want to choose *North by Northwest* like they're doing at the park?" asked Keisha. "Or maybe *Rear Window,* since you both prefer it?"

"I was thinking of something lighter. How about *The Karate Kid?*" I said as we walked into the library.

"Yes! Wait, which one?"

"I haven't seen the one with Jaden Smith, so let's start with that," I said.

"And then," Azalea appeared, holding the largest bowl of popcorn I had ever seen. "We're going to make sure you see something with Cary Grant next."

This time, it was my turn to squeal out a "Yes!"

"Sounds like a plan," said Keisha.

We settled in for a long night of movie marathons, popcorn, and eventually ordering a few too many pizzas. I had thought this was something needed mostly for Azalea, but as the three of us got into the movies and food, I realized it was something I had desperately needed as well.

Chapter Eight

In the morning, I gave Clover a quick walk before catching up with Azalea and Keisha in the kitchen. Azalea worked on getting breakfast together for Violet. Keisha had spent the night at the inn, sleeping on an air mattress in the kitchen. It was slightly ironic that all three of us had to stay in makeshift places when we were literally sleeping at a hotel, but it was still very much a startup business, and we all seemed to understand that there were sacrifices to be made. I hoped Azalea didn't have to make too many sacrifices to keep the business going.

Violet and Clover were chasing each other around the kitchen table. It was adorable to see how close the two of them had become in such a brief period of time.

"I have to figure out a way to get to the historical society today. I think they're open for a while this morning. And replace my phone. And somehow fix my car..." I rattled off the next steps of my to-do list. "I know I can walk a lot of these places, but I can't wait to have KG back in action."

"Don't forget that you can borrow my bike," said Keisha. She ran off to get it and brought it around to the porch outside the kitchen. I was grateful, but uncertain. The bike was a shiny emerald green with a matching helmet.

"Are you sure you won't need it?"

"Not if you bring it back before my shift ends tonight."

"Deal."

"You're going out?" asked Azalea.

"Is that okay? Anything I can do to help around here?" I asked.

"We're good. But I'll feel better once you have a phone with you again,"

Azalea said. "You're okay riding that thing?"

"Sure. You never forget how to ride a bike," I said.

Truth be told, it'd been years—if not decades—since I had last ridden a bike. They were popular to get around in D.C. these days, but the idea of darting through downtown traffic on a tiny metal thing without airbags always seemed to be asking for trouble. Not that KG had airbags, but at least it had a lot more cushioning to crunch if I got in an accident.

I must have proved to be the exception to the rule that you never forget how to ride a bike. I'm sure I looked like a prize with my inconsistent speed and constant stopping. Every time I hit a molehill, I fell, so eventually, I jumped off the bike and walked it over any potential issues on the road. Honestly, instead of making it quicker to go into town, I think the thing slowed me down.

The historical society was housed in a restored brick church. The building was fairly small, appearing to be a one-room chapel. A sign out front said that it dated back to the late 1800s. I tried the door, but it didn't budge. I glanced in one window not covered in stained glass and found it dark inside. I spotted a handwritten sign on the door apologizing for not being open today and offering special hours tomorrow to make up for it.

It was a few blocks to the cell phone store. The place wasn't a name-brand service store, but an independent electronics shop called "The Reboot," located near the end of the boardwalk stores. Going inside, I felt like I'd snuck into someone's attic. The cluttered shop was littered with electronics to be repaired, boxes of various products haphazardly stacked atop one another, and an oddly large number of clipboards. Half of the lights in the store were off, although that might have been because at least one overhead fluorescent light was as bright as a car's high beams. What I didn't see was anyone else.

"Hello?" I called out

"Coming! Coming!" A young woman appeared behind the desk. She must have been Keisha's older sister because she looked like a near photocopy of the teenager, although instead of wearing her hair in locs, she had intricate braids interlaced with colorful beads. "What can I help you with today?"

"Are you Desiree?" I couldn't resist checking.

"That would be me. Why? Are you looking for me?" She looked both eager and a touch concerned.

"Your sister Keisha works at my sister Azalea's inn."

"Oh, you must be Juniper. She mentioned you to me. Is she okay?" Desiree asked, visibly relaxing.

"Oh, yes, yes. People think Azalea and I are twins. I'm guessing that happens between you and Keisha a lot."

She chuckled. "Yeah, that's true."

"Keisha told me you are... were Tess's roommate? I'm very sorry for your loss."

Desiree took a step back from the desk and nodded. "It's been quite a shock. I'm going to miss her." The look of sadness that crossed her face nearly broke my heart.

I wondered how much to push. I really was here to get my phone replaced. Maybe I should have started with that. However, since I was here, I didn't want to pass up the opportunity that had fallen into my lap. "Keisha said that Tess was planning on moving out."

Desiree shook her head. "I was really surprised by that. Tess said it wasn't me, but she wouldn't tell me any details."

"Did she do anything unusual?"

Desiree shrugged and frowned. "She had changed. I don't know exactly why or when, but she spent all of her time either locked away in her room or out somewhere." She looked like she was holding back tears. "We used to spend all of our time together. I know it sounds middle schoolish, but we got friendship necklaces." She pulled the necklace out. It was half of a golden heart. I assumed Tess had worn the matching piece.

"I met her once, but she seemed really sweet."

"Yeah, A real heart of gold. She would give you the shirt off her back if she thought it'd make you happy. But she could get in these moods. Get really obsessive about things. There was the time she was going to become a full-time dog walker. You should have seen the pile of library books she'd gotten on dogs. She'd gotten as far as making a logo and website for the business. Then, just before she launched, she quit to start knitting baby blankets for preemies. In a two-week period, she made maybe 300 of them. I don't think she slept. But as soon as one of these obsessions took over, it'd suddenly fade away. That was Tess—all or nothing."

That resonated with me. Honestly, it sounded a lot like me. Before I got into library work, I tried on several careers. I went to three colleges before I finally graduated. Finding library work was such a relief. Suddenly, I had a job that allowed me to indulge every passing fancy. Need to escape to a new interest? I just had to open a book.

"Did this secret obsession involve Rory Walsh?" I asked.

A dark look passed over Desiree's face. "I have no idea, but what was a married man with a kid doing with a twenty-three-year-old? Have you asked your sister about that?"

"She honestly doesn't know." I paused, trying to decide on a different tactic. "Did Tess ever mention the *Book of Kells*? Or say why she was going to the cemetery?"

Desiree thought for a moment. "Not exactly. But *Kells*, yeah, that sounds familiar. I can't remember why. I want to say something about some family member. Sorry, I don't know. Did you just come in here to ask me all these questions?" Her patience was obviously wearing thin.

"No. I have a problem. I broke my phone." I held up the mangled mess of hard plastic and wires. Desiree cringed at the sight. I decided to butter her up a bit. "Keisha said you'd be the best one to bring this too." Okay, so maybe she hadn't actually said that, but I couldn't imagine she wouldn't.

That brought out a genuine smile. "Yeah, that's a mess alright. You looking to get a new one?" I looked back around the store with some hesitation. The place was dark and dusty. Could I trust a phone from here? Desiree must have sensed my concern. "I know this looks like someone's basement, but trust me, I'm sure I've got what you need somewhere in here. Plus, I'll hook you up with a fantastic warranty."

Within a half hour, Desiree had helped me select a new phone. It was a refurbished one, but it was new to me. Plus, the warranty did sound solid, and the price was surprisingly excellent. Best of all, she found all of my information backed up to the cloud and transferred it to the new phone.

I had been concerned that I'd have to change numbers since this wasn't a dealer, but she walked me through that process, so I could keep everything. New phone, old information.

Unfortunately, as soon as I finished setting up my phone, it sprang to life with an avalanche of missed calls, texts, and emails. Some were from Azalea, but the majority of them were from Greyson. It looked like he was taking his role as my new boss seriously. Too seriously.

"I need this Monday at 9:30 a.m—"

"Where are we with the update? I need information stat—"

"I know it's Friday night, but I need you to—"

"Why haven't you responded to anything, Juniper?!"

"I have heard nothing from you since Friday afternoon!"

"We need to have a serious talk—"

"Juniper—"

"Juniper—"

"Juniper!"

I couldn't deal with his lack of boundaries right now. If I had tried, I would probably have responded with a voicemail of me making a raspberry sound. Not exactly professional. Besides, I really didn't want to tell him about what was happening in Rose Mallow. Although, with the way the press was stationed outside the Calverton Foundation, it probably wouldn't take long for him to find out. I shuddered at the idea of what anyone at the Library of Congress might think, let alone Greyson. I put the phone on silent, slid it into my back pocket, and tried to pretend the thing didn't exist.

Before I left, Desiree pulled me aside and said, "Hey, do me a favor. If you find anything, let me know. And can you make sure my little sis stays out of trouble? I know she's probably buzzing with energy to help you out, but I don't want her getting hurt. I'm not sure I want her to keep working at the inn right now with Rory still missing."

I nodded. "Trust me, she couldn't be in a safer place. Azalea and I will keep an eye out for her."

I hopped back on Keisha's bike to return to the inn. I got a better feel of it and didn't give in to every bump in the road. As I tried to go with the flow, I forced my hunched-up shoulders to relax. I kept repeating a mantra of, "Kids bike, so can you," and worked hard to make myself go faster. It didn't help to be around more people in the small downtown area, who I suspected were all laughing at my obvious inabilities. One might think that spending summers in a former resort town would mean a lot of biking, but I had typically walked most places. When we got to be old enough, Azalea and I shared Nana Z's ancient but enormous town car. Driving that beast wasn't fun, but at least it provided us with some freedom.

My memories must have distracted me because I nearly jumped the curb and almost ran someone over. Out of everyone, it could be, of course, I almost hit Whitney Sullivan. She jumped backwards and plopped bottom-first onto the sidewalk. A bunch of flowers in her hand went flying.

"Are you psycho?" Whitney yelled. I jumped off the bike, letting it fall against the curb. When I tried to offer her a hand up, she cried out, "Get off of me! You almost killed me!"

"I'm sorry, I'm sorry," I replied. When she wouldn't accept my help, I ran to get the flowers that had fallen everywhere.

"Stop it! Leave them alone! You ruined them!" She gathered them up in her hand. They were all coral-colored roses, but they had gotten bruised and broken. "Great. What am I going to tell Granny?"

"I'm truly sorry. It was an awful accident. Please, let me buy you a new dozen."

Whitney looked at me suspiciously. She chewed her bottom lip and considered my request. "All right. Fine. But only because they're for Granny. They're her favorite color." She tossed the damaged roses into a nearby trash can, and we walked up the sidewalk to the florist. I pushed Keisha's bike beside me as we headed there.

As we walked, a memory tugged at me. "Whitney, how long has your family lived in Rose Mallow?" I remembered seeing "ó Súilleabháin" while at the Calverton Foundation, or maybe it had been on a gravestone at Tidewater Cemetery. I suspected that this was an older, more Irish way of writing Sullivan.

Whitney smiled a sincere smile. "My family was aboard the Dove when it docked at St. Mary's City in 1634. My ancestors were founding members of Rose Mallow a couple generations later."

"Wow. That's amazing. My family has been a bit more nomadic. We have an old family map going back several generations on my father's mother's side," I said.

"A map?" Whitney asked.

"Yeah, not exactly the traditional family tree. Nana Z's grandparents had left Germany to come to America at the turn of the century," I replied, gently guiding the bike as I walked alongside it.

"Did they come through Ellis Island?"

"No. They came to Locust Point in Baltimore. There was a time it was the second largest immigration station in the country," I said, thinking about the photos that Nana Z had shown of them when they first arrived in the city. They had lived in a brick rowhouse. Every weekend, my great-great-grandmother would wash the marble steps—the one luxury those early houses enjoyed. Nana Z recalled helping her on Sunday mornings. "But the map shows more than just Maryland and Europe. Some of my family remained in Germany until the 1930s."

Whitney made a face, realizing where I was going. "The Nazis?"

I nodded. "They were able to escape. They couldn't get visas to America, so they scattered to whatever country would take them. They ended up in some far-off places, like Buenos Aires and Shanghai."

Whitney cocked her head to the side. "Argentina and China? No kidding. Never would have guessed that."

"It's taken years, but Nana Z always marked the map with where our family ended up in the diaspora," I said with pride. Every time our ancestors had moved somewhere new, it was marked on the map with names and dates. I wondered where Azalea had put the map. Had she added herself and Violet to it?

"Diaspora?" she repeated.

"Jewish people around the world, living outside Israel," I defined.

"I didn't think you were particularly religious."

I shrugged. "Well, no, I guess not, but being Jewish still is part of my

84

identity."

"Then why do you care so much about a Catholic book?"

"The *Book of Kells*? Well, let me put it this way. They call Jews the 'People of the Book.' That means the Torah and other books of the Bible, but to me, it means recognizing how important books are. They're time capsules— connections to our ancestors and the world around us," I said with a smile.

Whitney nodded. "Was it the same for Nana Z? I mean, Rose Mallow doesn't exactly have a large Jewish community."

"It doesn't. Although, from what I've heard, it's growing at least a little. But I guess she was following our family's tradition of moving somewhere new. At least this time, it wasn't over an entire ocean," I replied with a laugh.

She said, "Granny has a gorgeous family tree going back at least twenty-five generations. It's hanging in her study. She's also the president of the Rose Mallow Historical Society and the Rose Mallow Genealogical Society."

I had to bite back a giggle, remembering her grandmother listing off her civic connections while threatening me unconvincingly with an umbrella. However, I sobered up when I realized that talking to her would be helpful.

"So, I know I got off on a bad foot with your granny, but, um, do you think you could arrange for us to chat? I'd love to learn more about Rose Mallow's history, including your family's history." My voice was far more sheepish than I had expected. I felt a blush creep across my face. We had reached the florist, and I used it as an excuse to turn away and lock up the bike.

Whitney laughed. She laughed so hard, I thought she'd start crying. It certainly wasn't the reaction I was expecting.

"Oh, that's a good one. You want to talk with Granny?" She wiped her eyes. Then she looked at me and studied me more deeply. "Wait, you're serious, aren't you?"

I nodded. Someone with that much history at her fingertips seemed worth getting over my anxieties about. Maybe she knew if there was any truth to this *Book of Kells* in Rose Mallow idea. We walked into the florist and quickly found another dozen coral-colored roses.

As we took them up to the register, Whitney said, "Okay, I'll arrange it, but this I have to watch. You can meet with her if I get to go with you." Not my favorite idea, but I nodded and shook her hand on it. Whitney promised to text me with a time. I wasn't crazy about sharing my cell phone number with her, but like with the proposed meeting with Cordelia Sullivan, it seemed worth the opportunity.

By the time I got back to the inn and returned the bike, it was mid-afternoon. Azalea was literally racing through the house. She flew by me so quickly, I almost thought she was on roller skates.

"Do you need help?" I asked as she passed by again.

"I'm getting Vi's lunch taken care of. And then getting some items up to the guests. And then..." She counted off her list on her fingers.

"Why don't I take the guest items upstairs?"

"I've got it," said Keisha. She carried a tall stack of pillows and blankets. "And I've already gotten Vi fed. She's watching TV, and I'll be right back to watch her. We're under control here. Juniper, I also walked Clover and gave him a snack."

"Thanks, Keisha," I said.

"Okay, then, I'm going to water the garden," said Azalea as she headed toward the door.

Keisha paused on the staircase. "Sprinklers are already set. And I think we're due for rain tomorrow." She continued upwards.

"Great. Then I'll do some cleaning." She ran her hands along a panel and looked upset to find that it wasn't dusty.

"Cleaned earlier," Keisha's voice resonated from upstairs.

"Good, good. Then I'll work on organizing the Carriage House," She sprinted down the hallway, but I reached out and grabbed her.

"Azalea, stop doing this to yourself," I said.

"No stopping here," she replied with a too-large smile. She tried pulling away from me. I grabbed her tighter. "There's too much to do."

I pulled her close to me and hugged her tightly. "We're going to figure this out, Azalea. I promise. We will find out what happened."

She stopped fussing. I thought she was settling down, but then she whispered into my ear, "Juniper, do you...do you think Rory could have done this? Do you think he hurt that young woman?"

"No." I didn't know what I believed at the moment, but I knew what my sister needed to hear. "There is no way in a million years that Rory would ever hurt her. Or anyone else."

She nodded but didn't appear convinced. "I want to think that too, but…" She gently pulled away and opened a trash can. Inside were the remnants of crushed flowers. They were so smashed and bruised that I couldn't tell what kind of flower they were or what color they used to be.

I examined them more closely. There was a small piece of paper stuck in between some petals. As I pulled it out, I saw it was just a corner of a paper. The thickness suggested it was from a card that had probably come with the flowers.

"Was there a note with these?"

Azalea shook her head. So, this must be a remnant. I studied it and saw what looked like part of an embossed silver curve. Below it was a bit of purple ink. I could just make out the tops of a few letters, what I thought might be "GEO." Maybe for the word "geography"? "Geothermal"? I wasn't sure. I thought about running into Whitney at the flower shop. Maybe I needed to go back to the store to see if they could tell me anything. With my new-to-me phone, I took photos of the scrap and the mess.

"When did you find these?"

"Not long ago. They were on the back of the porch."

"Have you told the police?" I asked.

She shook her head.

"If he did this, then maybe examining these flowers could help them find him," I said.

She considered the idea. "Maybe. But maybe it'll convince them more that he hurt that poor girl."

"Oh, Azalea. I'm so sorry. But even if he left you these crushed flowers, that doesn't mean he hurt anyone. Will you tell them?"

"I'll think about it," she said as she plopped down on the floor. "Honestly, I don't know what to think anymore. Keisha had talked about organizing a search party. I want to, but I…" Her voice trailed off.

"That's a great idea," I said and then added, "for the rest of us to handle."

Azalea walked out of the room, and I followed her into the kitchen. She curled up on a chair next to Violet, who happily watched some brightly colored cartoons on the kitchen television set. Clover played with a squeaky toy underneath the table. I figured that was also courtesy of Keisha.

"Juniper, what can you tell me about the *Book of Kells*? Why was Rory involved with that?" Azalea asked.

I turned on the kettle and pulled out her collection of tea. "I can tell you the history of the book. And I can tell you about the rumors that a valuable part of the Kells might have come to Maryland. But I don't know how or why Rory would have been involved."

I explained the history as best as I could. Azalea had heard of them, but she didn't know why anyone would have thought they were connected to Rose Mallow.

"Honestly, I don't know how that isn't fanciful thinking," I said. "I mean, I get the idea. Rose Mallow was founded around the same time as war was breaking out in Ireland and England. The monks moved *Kells* to Dublin, thinking they'd be safer there. Maybe someone thought that they'd be safer coming to America. But the covers had already been missing for hundreds of years."

"So you don't think this is real?" she asked as she played with Violet's hair.

"I guess it's possible that the covers had been kept hidden. Maybe they had been stolen, and like the books themselves, perhaps they were recovered. Maybe someone thought it'd be better to keep their return secret. But I'm a reference librarian. I don't believe things because I want to, or because it would be simpler to do so," I explained. Azalea nodded. The tea was ready, and I poured her a mug. I didn't get one for myself. As much as settling down with a hot cup sounded pleasant, I had some other things I wanted to check out before the day ended.

I asked Azalea, "Where was Rory staying? Since the...you know—"

"The divorce proceedings started? Well, he was in between places, so he's been staying at a hotel on the outskirts of town. I think the police already searched there." She gently pushed Violet off her lap, got up, and dug into one of the kitchen drawers. "I haven't told anyone else this, but I've got a key."

I popped an eyebrow. Azalea batted my thoughts away. "Nothing like that. We aren't getting back together. It's because of Violet. We're trying to keep things amicable. Or at least I was." She stared out the back door, and I knew she was picturing the crushed flowers.

"You didn't tell Detective Gupta about the key?" She shook her head.

"Not Deputy Torres either?"

She breathed in deeply. "I haven't told them about it. Yet. They've been there already. What do they need a key for?"

She walked over and dangled the key in front of me. "Look, I'm not asking you to do anything. But you sometimes see things others miss. This is yours if it's helpful." She placed the key on the countertop, along with her car keys, and went back to Violet. I stared at each for a few moments before pocketing both.

Chapter Nine

I decided the car keys were permission to borrow Azalea's minivan. Compared to my tiny KG, the minivan felt like steering a behemoth, and I was almost as unsteady driving it as I had been riding Keisha's bike. However, nowhere in or around town was far away, so I got it safely parked in the town center.

I stopped at the Purple Oyster to check on Harmony. Before I could order, Harmony spotted me and pulled me aside. She ushered me to a small table while I looked back longingly at the displays of scones and muffins. My stomach protested loudly about being away from them.

"Why were you at the cemetery?" Harmony asked.

I debated what to tell her. When I last saw her at Tidewater Cemetery, she was spouting something about a family curse. I assumed she was overcome with grief, but I wasn't sure how she would take the rest of the story. But Harmony was Tess's aunt. She deserved to know everything.

"I work at the Library of Congress as a reference librarian. I specialize in rare books. Rory called me because he'd found this diary that had something to do with the *Book of Kells*. I was intrigued enough that I went there on Friday night to see it." I paused before adding, "He called it the O'Doyle diary."

Harmony's head dropped. A waterfall of frizzy red hair cascaded around her. "I know that diary," she said softly. I sat up straighter. "Honestly, I should've burned it years ago."

"Is that part of the curse you mentioned?"

She sighed and looked back up. I followed her gaze out a side window.

The Chesapeake Bay looked so peaceful. "Our family came to this country a long time ago from Ireland. We were one of the first to arrive in the 1600s. However, my ancestors brought darkness with them. Some say they made an evil deal to escape the English."

"The curse?" I asked.

She nodded. "We've had so many sadnesses over the years. My sister, my father, and now my niece. But the curse goes back much earlier."

"And you think the diary carries that curse?"

"Yes," replied Harmony. "Sure, the O'Doyle diary's a treasured heirloom, blah, blah, blah. But it's brought nothing but trouble. I've tried hiding it before, but somehow, someone always finds it."

"Did Tess find the diary?" I asked.

"She must have. I locked it away years ago."

"But why was Rory involved?"

"I don't know what they were up to, but it was no good. He must have poisoned her brain with some idea or scheme or something. I just know it," she said.

"Why do you say that? How did they know each other?" I asked.

Harmony shook her head. "Tess was a kid. I don't know what they were doing together, but he's older than her and married. Whatever they were up to couldn't have been good."

I disagreed, but I didn't have any more proof than she did. Either way, I wasn't going to badger a grieving aunt. I thought about my talk with Desiree and changed tactics. "Had you noticed any changes in Tess lately?"

Harmony sighed. She considered my question. "I should have paid more attention. Ever since her mom died, I tried to keep her under my wing, but she was growing up. I couldn't hold my little butterfly back anymore."

"May I ask how her mom passed away?"

"Cancer. Diagnosed one day and gone less than a month later. Broke all our hearts, but I'm glad she didn't suffer."

"That must have been devastating. What about her father?"

"Deadbeat disappeared years ago."

I pushed further. "And her grandfather?"

She stood up suddenly. I could feel a change in her demeanor. Instead of quiet and resigned, an anger festered. I had prodded too much. "That diary is the reason my father—Tess's grandfather—is dead. It's the reason she's dead. If someone doesn't find it and destroy it, it's going to kill again."

"What do you mean?" I wanted to ask more, but Harmony was shaking her head. In fact, her whole body appeared to be shuddering or twitching. I hadn't meant to set her off, but my questions have obviously touched a nerve.

"Sometimes the past should stay in the past," she said.

One phrase etched in the upper register of the National Archives in D.C. sprung into my mind, "What's past is prologue." If I recall correctly, it was a line from Shakespeare. I wondered how this diary could have caused such grief.

"This diary's very old, but has it been in your family the whole time?" I asked.

"Probably. I assume that's why it was called the O'Doyle diary. My father couldn't let go of the idea of finding the *Kells'* covers. My mother said he was bewitched by the diary. She never got over his death and always blamed that diary. She called it cursed. I should've listened to her. For a time, I was also entranced by the thing, but I broke free of its pull."

"How'd you do that?"

Harmony closed her eyes. "It wasn't easy. I spent a good part of my teens and twenties trying to complete my father's search for the *Book of Kells'* missing covers. I pored over the O'Doyle diary for clues, but I never found anything. It took my mother's dying wish to break me of its spell. She told me to destroy the diary, but I locked it away instead. I thought doing that was enough. But Tess must have found that cursed book anyway."

"How did your father die?" I asked.

"How do you think? From that thing. That poisonous, wretched thing." Her eyes darkened as she spoke.

"I don't understand. Are you saying the O'Doyle diary somehow killed him?" I couldn't hold back making a face on how ridiculous this idea was.

She stuck out a finger at me. "Fine, don't believe me. But my father's gone, my niece's gone, and your sister's husband is missing. All because of that damn diary. You keep asking all these questions, and watch out, because you might be next."

"I'm sorry, what?" I asked. I didn't think Harmony was threatening me, but she was clearly worked up.

"You can't leave this alone, can you? You know why? Because that vile curse is extending itself to you. Well, I won't let you contaminate me any further. I've renounced that thing." She shuddered before standing up and waltzing away.

To my utter surprise, Harmony then climbed up on top of a countertop and shouted to the room. "The Purple Oyster's now closed."

People in the restaurant whispered to each other. A few stood up, but no one seemed certain what they should do. I looked over at the couple of employees behind the counter, who were also shrugging with uncertainty. This apparently angered Harmony further, so she outright shouted, "We're closed. Go home. Now."

After a few moments of murmuring, people got up to go. I filed out with everyone else. As I did so, I looked back to see Harmony sending her staff away. I waited outside, but within a few minutes, all the lights went off inside the Purple Oyster. I overheard people grumbling and complaining about the sudden change. A few remarked on how much worse Harmony's moods had become. I hesitated outside the place, still deciding what to do next. When I peeked into a window, I saw Harmony sitting alone at a table in the darkened building. She gazed out, staring at the Chesapeake Bay.

I walked the boardwalk, checking out which stores and restaurants had survived since I was last here and which ones were new. I recognized an old, new-age crystal shop and a used bookstore. Squeezed in the two between was a place with brown paper covering the windows and a poster proclaiming that something was coming soon, although it didn't specify what. An old-fashioned ice cream parlor had been transformed into a serve-yourself frozen yogurt place. I thought about going there to ease my rumbling stomach, but decided it wasn't worth the sugar crash that would inevitably follow.

I also wasn't interested in popping into the Indigo Room restaurant, which looked like a place where a meal might cost the same as a mortgage payment.

I slapped my forehead. Wasn't I supposed to get together with Leo there? We hadn't nailed down the plans, and I didn't have his number. Since my phone had been on the fritz then, I hadn't given him mine either. It'd been so long since I had last gone on a date, that I tried convincing myself it didn't matter if I waited a bit longer.

I sat on an empty bench that faced the water. Families and couples wandered by. Occasionally, a jogger braved the blistering sun. At least the Chesapeake Bay provided a little relief with a smattering of breezes cooled over the water. I looked to my right, trying to make out how far the boardwalk stretched south. Somewhere, a mile or so down, it ran behind the Wildflower Inn. A mile beyond that was Redbud Park, where we had missed Movie Night last night.

When I gazed to my left, there wasn't much further to go. The boardwalk ended just past the Purple Oyster. After that, it was a mix of rocky terrain and private properties. Along the waterfront, homes were expensive—whether they were in the historic area like the Wildflower Inn or the more modern ones to the north of the downtown area. However, I knew I wouldn't have to go much inland before prices dropped considerably. Outside of this sliver, there wasn't much wealth in the area. Rose Mallow was a place of contrasts. Then again, so was D.C. I wondered if any place wasn't these days.

"I didn't expect to run into you," said a voice behind me. I turned to find Detective Gupta with a cup of frozen yogurt. She wasn't in a suit but a sleeveless blouse over some cropped yoga pants. She spotted me eyeing her fro-yo cup. "Raspberry sorbet. One of my favorites."

"Good choice." I scooted along the bench to make room for her.

"Yeah, I needed it after a good workout. Have you been to the new fitness center? The converted barn?" She gestured to the north somewhere. I shook my head. "That's right. You don't live around here."

"It's been a long time since I've been back to Rose Mallow."

"I should probably ask you about that, but I am officially off the clock for the moment," she said with a laugh.

"Does that mean I shouldn't call you Detective right now?"

"Lakshmi works if I can call you Juniper?"

"Sounds like a deal," I said. "Assuming this is allowed?"

"What wouldn't be allowed? Talking?" She cocked her head to the side. Her spoon hovered in mid-air.

"With an active case. I mean, have you found out anything more about Rory?"

"Okay, so maybe talking about the case isn't a good idea. But we can talk about other things," she replied.

"Like what?"

"Well, how does Rose Mallow compare to when you were last here?"

I looked back out at the Bay. "Some things don't change. This view is the same. The boardwalk has a few new places, like the fro-yo shop, but mostly it's the same. I don't know. So much of Rose Mallow feels like…" I thought for a moment, trying to piece together the right words. "Like a snow globe."

"A snow globe?" She arched an eyebrow.

"Frozen in time. Most everything is the same here as it's been for decades. Well, no, not that it's all exactly the same. Certainly, having my sister run my grandmother's house as an inn is definitely different," I said. "And I don't remember you being here before. Did you grow up in the area?"

"No. I lived in Howard County and worked in Baltimore. Both the county and the city. We came down here for a slower pace of life. Thought it'd be a good change of pace." Lakshmi scooped at her sorbet. I hoped she didn't hear my stomach growling.

"We? Are you married?"

She nodded. "Yeah. Have two kids. Your requisite boy and girl pairing."

"Nice. How old?"

"Twins. They're in elementary school. It's been nice for them, being here on the water." We both stared out at the waves. There were a few sailboats touring around. It must have been nice to be out there right now. "What about you? Married? Kids?"

"Not sure if I want to get married."

"Because of Azalea and Rory's break up?"

"Maybe. I don't know." My parents were still married, although I sometimes wondered why, given the way they constantly bickered at each other. I sort of remembered my grandfather, and I think he and Nana Z had a happy marriage, but I wasn't sure. She hadn't talked about him much after he died. I guess the real question was if I was truly ready to settle down or not. I had a good job and a townhouse, but I still had a bit of a wandering streak in me.

"Well, I'm a fan," she said.

"Of marriage?"

"Yep." She put the empty cup down on the bench between us.

"What does your spouse do?"

She smiled. "Why, he's a librarian."

I couldn't help laughing. "Really?"

"For the public library system, though. He's an assistant branch manager. I think you'd like him, although he's much more about science fiction and fantasy than rare books," she said.

"Hey, I like science fiction and fantasy too."

"Great. Personally, I'm more into mysteries. Especially Laura Lippman."

"Because of how many of her books take place in Maryland?" I asked.

"Doesn't hurt."

I realized I enjoyed talking to Lakshmi far more than I could have expected. This bright, relaxed woman was so different from her stoic detective persona. However, I couldn't help wondering which one I'd see the next time she was back in a suit.

"How's your sister holding up?" she asked.

"Oh, you know. I think it hits her in waves," I said, thinking about Azalea cleaning the house earlier. Maybe I shouldn't have left her there. Not that I would do much good sitting around the Wildflower Inn and waiting by the phone, but that seemed to be what I had left her to do.

"I'm sorry. I'm sure it's been hard since they split."

"Well, yeah. They have a daughter, and she has a new business. It's been a lot for her to manage," I said. "My heart's really heavy for her."

"I can imagine. I'd feel the same way if this was happening to my sister."

"You have a sister?" I asked.

"Three of them. And I'm the oldest. So, I feel responsible for them, especially when they're having a hard time. Trust me, with four girls, one of us is always facing some sort of issue." She smiled as she spoke, but there was a tone in her voice that suggested she had seen her share of "issues."

"Yeah, I think Azalea felt that way about me until I started working for the Library of Congress. She always worried about how I'd make ends meet." I shook my head, remembering the emails and phone calls from her. She worried more than our mother.

"And now the tables are reversed, huh?"

"I suppose so. I wish I could make everything better for her."

"All that stress. Especially with that mountain of bills. Must be a lot," Lakshmi said.

"It is..." I paused. "Wait, you know about the bills?"

"I know some things," Lakshmi replied. The poker face had returned.

"Like what?"

"Like that she's in danger of losing the Wildflower Inn. I also know that Rory had been out of steady work for a while before getting the dealership job, but that doesn't exactly pay well. But, they both have sizable life insurance policies." She tried to make it sound casual, but I was beginning to wonder if this chance encounter was even that.

"I'm sure that's because of Violet."

"I'm sure it is," she said, but it didn't sound like she believed that.

"Are you accusing Azalea of something?"

Lakshmi threw her hands up in mock surrender. "I'm just talking about issues."

"And I didn't think we were supposed to discuss the case. That you were off the clock."

She shrugged. "Either way, the clock's ticking. The first 48 hours a person is missing are the most important. We're nearing the end of that time period."

"Azalea would never hurt Rory, if that's what you're suggesting." I had to work to control my voice.

"I'm not suggesting anything. I'm just asking questions," Lakshmi said.

"Why would Azalea hurt Rory? Or Tess?" I asked.

"Along those same lines, let me throw a question back at you," she said.

"Why was Rory involved with Tess?"

"Involved? You think he was dating Tess?" I asked. I thought about Desiree asking practically the same question at The Reboot.

Lakshmi shrugged and took another bite of her sorbet. Then she asked, "How do you think Azalea handled that? Seeing her husband divorce her to run off with someone younger and without any kids?"

My mouth went dry. I felt the flames shooting up through my body. It took every ounce of self-control I could muster to not let loose on the detective about how ridiculous her question was. The idea that Rory would leave Azalea for Tess and that Azalea would retaliate by killing Tess and who knows what with Rory? Absolutely impossible. I closed my eyes and tried to calm myself down. It didn't work, but it brought up another thought.

"Is any of what you told me true?" I asked.

She looked genuinely surprised at my question. "What?"

"Your marriage? Your twins? The library?" I stood up. I was shaking.

"Of course, it's true," she said. "Or well, most of it. Look, I just want to do my job. And I think you want me to do it too. I know you want to know where Rory is."

"Then stop wasting time on Azalea."

I didn't wait for her to respond. Instead, I stormed off the boardwalk. It was time for me to stop wasting time as well. We would not be friends. I couldn't think of her as sorbet-loving, gym-going Lakshmi. If Detective Gupta wouldn't focus on finding Tess's actual killer, then obviously, she needed my help.

Chapter Ten

Stopping for fast food wasn't my favorite choice, but I needed something quick and easy. Plus, the closest options were out near where the hotels were. Honestly, hotel was too nice of a word for the place where Rory had been staying. When I first drove up to it, I thought the place was abandoned. Half of the parking lot lights were out, and there were just a few turned on around and inside the long, squat two-story building. The place looked like it dated back at least sixty years and probably hadn't been painted often since it was constructed. A sign saying "OTEL" was the only identification for the place. I hoped that the place was at least cheap.

I climbed up to the second floor and followed the exterior hallway down to Rory's room. His room had some signs saying KEEP OUT. I assumed they were left there by the police. However, I didn't come out here to not at least peek inside. I attempted looking through a window, but the blinds were too far down for me to see anything.

"Hey! Hey!" An older woman appeared at her doorstep. She looked like she was in her seventies. She had long silvery hair and enormous silver hoop earrings. She wore a tight black shirt with dark jeans and the largest silver belt buckle I'd ever seen, encrusted with turquoise. She wasn't wearing boots, though, but five-inch black heels. I hoped to be as stylish as her one day.

"Excuse me?"

"You need to leave that guy alone." She placed her hands on her hips and leaned back against her door jamb. She seemed far too upscale for this place.

"What do you mean?"

"I've had enough of you coming back and forth all hours of the day and night. And then all those police come thundering through." She switched to crossing her arms across her chest. I spotted a few tattoos peeking out from under her arms.

"I think you have me confused with someone else. I haven't been here before. Ever."

The woman looked uncertain. "Hang on." She disappeared inside and reappeared moments later wearing glasses. I liked their bright teal frame. "Okay, okay, I see now. You do look different from that other woman."

"How?" I asked, hoping to keep her talking.

"Well, you both have short hair, but hers was spikier. And I think it might have been purple. Or blue. She was taller than you, and excuse me for saying, but a bit younger too." She had to be describing Tess. More and more, it appeared that she and Rory were involved somehow. Were they dating? Or was it something else? Obviously, they had made some sort of connection with the O'Doyle diary. Whose idea had it been to give the diary to Orson Bradford?

"Did you know the man who was staying here well?" I asked.

She considered my question for a few beats and said, "He hadn't been here all that long. I've been coming here for decades. See, guys like him come and go. Sure, he seems nice. Smiles and waves and all that jazz, but people don't come here for good reasons."

"Why do you say that?" I asked, wondering if she counted herself in that consideration.

"Seen enough happen that ain't good. This isn't the first time a door's been covered in police tape, and I don't think it'll be the last." She paused. "Why are you here?"

"Trying to find him."

"What? He owe you money? Drugs?"

I shook my head. "He's married to my sister."

"Oh, that's rich. You getting on with her husband."

"What? He's missing, and I'm trying to find him. For her."

"Look, honey, let me give you a piece of advice." She relaxed against the door jamb and kept her hands in her tight jeans pockets. "People who come around here to this dump…. They don't want to be found."

Before she said anything else, I heard a man's voice in the background. "Hey, Gladys, who you talking to? Get back in here." She shrugged and slammed shut the door. I had been dismissed.

"Well, good day to you, Gladys."

Left on my own, I considered if I should violate the police's keep-out signs or not. I didn't want to get in trouble, or worse, mess up the room for them. But then I thought about Azalea. Maybe I could bring a different view to things. I looked around. No one else seemed to be out, and the only camera in sight was broken with the lens smashed. If there was any other sign of security, I didn't see it, and given the condition of the place, I felt fairly confident that I was safe. Besides, I was already up here, so someone would probably ask as is. I decided to just spend three minutes inside.

At least I had brought some gloves with me. I slipped inside the room and felt a complete and utter letdown. The small room consisted of two made beds, a dresser, and a TV. Nothing looked touched. Not even the linens were askew. It was like no one had stayed here at all. At least in the bathroom, I found a duffel bag with some wrinkled clothes and a few toiletries, but they didn't strike me as anything important.

I tried the hotel safe, trying to determine what four number code Rory could have used. First, I tried Violet's birthday. Nothing. I tried his birthday. Nada. I sat there for a few moments before attempting Azalea's birthday. The safe popped open. That was a bit of a surprise, but at least it worked. Unfortunately, whatever had been inside the safe was now gone. I may have uttered a few choice words when finding it empty.

I attempted the closet, opening drawers, looking under pillows. Anything I could think of. My three minutes had already passed, and I needed to leave soon. I wasn't sure that Gladys next door wouldn't call the cops, and I didn't want to try explaining my actions to Detective Gupta or Deputy Torres.

Not that I really could explain my actions to myself, either. Had I really thought I was so special that I could find something they hadn't? What had I expected? That the O'Doyle diary would just be sitting around here, waiting for me? Anger bubbled up within me. I was mad at this being a bust. Mad at

Rory for disappearing. Mad at myself for letting Azalea down. My hands locked into fists, and no matter how much I tried to tamp down the feeling, it surged through me. Without an outlet, I kicked hard at one of the beds. It rattled, and I jumped back, scared that I had somehow hurt it. Then I noticed something had fallen from behind the bed frame. The edge of a paper peeked out. I picked at it until I pulled it out from back there.

However, it still wasn't a diary or map or anything old at all. It was a small series of photos of Rory and Tess like you'd get from a photobooth. In most images, they made silly faces, but in the last one, they were smiling up at the camera with an arm wrapped around the other. I flipped it over, but there was nothing on the back.

"What're you doing, Rory?" I asked the photo. Of course, the answer was right there in front of me. They were a couple. That had to be the case. Maybe that's why Azalea and Rory had started divorce proceedings. I didn't want to ask my sister, but I needed to know. I pocketed the photo. This must have been why Rory asked me about the covers. He had to have been searching for them with Tess.

Back at the inn, Keisha was working at the front desk. She looked exhausted. One hand propped up her head, while the other rested on the counter in front of a laptop. She stared off into space.

"Are you okay?" I asked her.

"Yeah, of course," she replied, trying to perk up, but then a yawn escaped. "Oh, sorry. It's been a long day."

I looked at the clock on the wall. "You've been here a long time today. When does your shift finish?"

"I'm spending the night again. Staying with Vi and Clover. We're having a sleepover," she said with a tired smile.

"You don't have to stay," I said.

"I know, but it feels like something I can do to help Azalea and Vi," Keisha replied.

"That's nice of you. Where are they?"

"Azalea has them. Maybe giving them a bath together. Anyway, I'm helping with the search party for Rory. Tomorrow afternoon at the cemetery."

"Didn't the police already search there?" I asked.

"Yeah, but my sister and a bunch of her friends thought it'd be a good place to start. Rose Mallow has such a tiny police force. Desiree said that even if the county pitches in, we could be extra eyes. She asked me to manage the social media for the search."

I thought about how the weekend was almost over. There was no way I was leaving Azalea and going back to the Library of Congress tomorrow. Now that I had my phone back, I needed to let Greyson know. I hoped he didn't use that as an excuse to fire me.

"I should have started working on it sooner," Keisha said.

"Do you need help?" I came around to the back of the counter. She had several tabs open on her laptop, including an event page on a social media site, a map of the cemetery, and a webpage all about the event.

"It's pretty much all done. Although some people are pretty unhappy because they think Rory was involved with Tess's murder."

"What do you think?" I asked.

"I don't think he was involved."

"Why are you so certain?"

Keisha opened a few more tabs. "Well, I've been piecing together some threads online, but nothing concrete yet."

"What threads?"

"Well, I think one of them was up to something. Let me get back to you," Keisha said.

"Do the police know you're looking at this?" I wasn't crazy about Keisha's digital sleuthing on her own. If she could find something, there seemed just as good of a chance that someone could find her.

"No. Neither does Azalea. Or Desiree. I don't want anyone to worry until I have something definitive."

"You should leave this to the experts. I don't want you getting hurt."

Keisha's expression soured. "Oh, you mean like how you're leaving it to the experts?"

"What?"

"I know you've been asking and poking around. So, it's totally hypocritical for you to ask me to stop." I think she punched a few keys on the laptop hard for good measure. I got a quick peek at a few windows, most of which looked like forums. Unfortunately, I didn't get to see further before she closed the browser.

"Well, here's the difference. I'm an adult. Legally. If you get hurt, Azalea and I are going to be held responsible for you. Your family will never, ever forgive us, and we will never forgive ourselves."

Keisha pouted and replied, "You're a *librarian*, not a detective."

"Look, Azalea asked me to look into it."

"I love your sister, but even I can see she's obviously not in her right mind."

I immediately looked around to make sure Azalea didn't hear that. I leaned closer to Keisha and said, "That may be true, but it's because she's grieving. She was already grieving because of the divorce, and now she's grieving because Rory is missing. That's why I'm trying to help."

"And the same for me."

We were ending up in circles. I threw my hands up in surrender.

"I think part of this is that we're all exhausted. I'm going to bed, and I think you should, too." I stood there and waited. Keisha made a few sounds of exasperation, but after half a minute, she powered down the laptop. "Put it away somewhere. Come back in the morning with a fresh mind. At least that's what I am going to do."

I decided to leave Greyson a message letting him know that I wouldn't be at work this week. It was late, but to my surprise, he picked up the phone.

"Greyson Patterson speaking. Who is this?" he asked.

"Hey, Greyson, it's Juniper."

"Juniper, where have you been? I've been trying to reach you all weekend."

"I don't work on the weekend, plus I've had a family emergency."

Before I could explain further, he interrupted me to say, "I need you to come in early tomorrow. And plan to stay late. There's this big deadline coming up on the Dashiell Hammett collection for the new exhibit."

"Did you hear me? I have a family emergency. I was calling to say I won't be in for a while. At least a few days."

104

"That's not acceptable, Juniper. You didn't ask for the time off before disappearing on Friday. I've been making up for your mess all weekend."

"But Greyson…"

"Don't 'But Greyson' me. I need you in the office first thing tomorrow." It sounded like he didn't believe that my emergency was real. I had never "cried wolf" before, so I couldn't understand why he would act this way. Ever since he went from being my colleague to my boss, it had been just one power trip after another.

"My brother-in-law is…"

"Tomorrow morning. Nine a.m. No, wait, make that seven a.m. sharp. Otherwise, I'm putting in a report to HR."

"Wait, but Greyson…"

The line was dead. He had hung up on me. I stared at my cell phone. To use Nana Z's phrase, Greyson was very much a "shlemiel," but I hadn't expected him to be so unreasonable. I sighed. I loved the Library of Congress, but I felt stuck working for such someone with so much "chutzpah," to use another one of Nana Z's favorite words.

After all my time traveling around the world, I'd expected my work at the Library of Congress to be the culmination of my journeys. In some ways, it was. Every day, I had access to one of the best collections of books in the entire world. People treated me with respect when I told them that I worked there.

Yet, the truth was that I felt like little more than a cog in a big machine. I didn't get the freedom to work on the projects I wanted. Many of my duties were fairly mundane. Digitizing papers and cataloging them in a database was important work, but I found myself struggling. The work was exacting, and I made mistakes more often than I'd like to admit.

What could I do though? It felt trite to complain about a decent job at such an important place. I mean, sure, having a frustrating boss was difficult, but that could happen anywhere, right? And it wasn't like there were lots of opportunities for rare book librarians. Mine was a fairly specialized field of work.

Nonetheless, I knew one thing. Greyson was going to be disappointed. I couldn't abandon my sister now. Ever since Nana Z died, my job had been an easy excuse to explain why I never made it back to Rose Mallow to see her or Violet. I'd used it as a mask to cover my grief. I wasn't going to make that mistake again. Not even working at the great Library of Congress was more important than being here for Azalea now.

Chapter Eleven

As exhausted as I felt, I was up early. Azalea must have been up earlier. Her hair was askew, and her face was red and puffy. She was in the same place I'd found Keisha last night. She had a stack of fliers for the search party printed beside her, along with about four different coffee mugs and several small plates littered with crumbs. Seeing me, she thrust about half of the stack across the countertop at me.

"Juniper, great, great. Will you put these up around town?" I took the top one and looked over the details. The search party was going to start in the early afternoon around the cemetery. "Keisha put this all together. She's such a whiz with all of this. Oh, hey, do you want a muffin? I was up and baked a few dozen batches for the searchers." She waved behind her towards where several baskets sat, overflowing with muffins. "There's blueberry, chocolate, banana nut, corn. I didn't make bran, because who really likes bran, anyway? Although it's probably the healthiest for you."

I came around the back of the countertop and put a hand on her shoulder. She didn't stop me. However, we were interrupted by the trudge of the Chronos Channel TV crew coming down the stairs. I realized I hadn't seen them since yesterday after the announcement. We must have been on different schedules.

"Ashley," I called out. She came over with a few yawns. "Are you all heading out?"

"Yep. We've been given some cryptic info by Orson."

"Oh? Like what?"

"I don't exactly know. But he wants us to come back to the Calverton

Foundation."

The goateed guy came over. I thought I remembered Ashley had said he was named Jeremy. Or was it Eric? He added, "Yeah, that detective came to see us yesterday. She wanted to know all about Orson's claim about the O'Doyle diary. I think she was pretty disappointed that he didn't have it in hand."

"I wonder where it is," said Ashley. "He has some pictures from it and of that map. I think he's convinced that everything is at the golf course or somewhere near there."

"He thinks the covers are buried at the golf course?"

They both shrugged.

"Do you know how he got the, uh, scans?" I asked.

"No. Just that it convinced the bigwigs at Chronos to bring us all out for this. If it looks like it'll lead to something, we may stay longer or come back," Jeremy/Eric replied.

As he talked, Ruth appeared. "What are we mulling around here for? We're going to be late."

I turned to the group and asked, "Would it be okay if I joined you?"

Ruth jerked around and said, "Absolutely not." She crossed her arms across her chest. Ashley and Jeremy rolled their eyes simultaneously. I saw the tall man—wait, that one was Eric, if I remembered correctly—shake his head in the back. After Ruth tottered off to wherever, Eric popped over to me.

"Don't listen to her. I heard you're an expert on rare books."

"Well, yeah, I'm a librarian with the Library of Congress." I could explain in far greater detail, but I knew that name drop sufficed for most people.

"And you're somehow connected to all of this drama? To the murder and the disappearance?"

"I wouldn't say connected."

He waved his hands. "Anyway, I think we should interview you. On camera."

"Oh, I don't know about that." I wasn't sure what the higher-ups at the Library of Congress would think about it either. I could only imagine what Greyson was going to think when I emailed explaining why I wasn't going to make his deadline. I suspected that I'd be getting many calls from him and then probably from HR. I reassured myself that being here now was more important than meeting his inane demands.

"It'd give you a good excuse to be there today." He told me where to meet them and slipped me an extra media pass. I appreciated the gesture.

I still hadn't got KG's tires fixed, and Azalea needed her minivan today, but Keisha had left her bike for me. I had nicknamed the green bicycle "Wizard" in honor of the Wizard of Oz at the Emerald City. "If we're going to become friends," I told Wizard, "I figured it'd be good for you to have a name." With renewed confidence, I set out, trying to improve on my horrific biking skills.

The sky was cloudy, and there was a forecast for rain. I welcomed anything that might break the summer humidity, but I wondered how that might impact today's TV shoot. The golf course was much farther away from the inn than going downtown, but most of the roads out to it were pretty straight and flat. That helped me experiment with speed and gliding. I kept to the side of the road, afraid that I wasn't yet ready to escape a sudden car. Amazingly, I made it to the site without incident.

Although there wasn't a press conference scheduled for today, I still had to wind through a few scattered media vehicles outside the gate. At first, no one realized who I was, but then someone recognized me, and all the remaining reporters ran after me, waving their arms and yelling out questions about Tess and Rory.

Rain spit on all of us. Not enough to warrant an umbrella, but enough that I grew concerned about my clumsy riding and dodging the group. I went as quickly as I could on Wizard, silently cajoling the bike to speed faster but safely. A gauntlet formed, and I wasn't sure I'd make it.

"Can you tell us what you were doing—"

"How did you know—"

"Do you think the Kells' covers are really—"

I tried ignoring their shouts and continued towards the gate. I maneuvered around wires jutting from their vans and weaved through a series of outstretched microphones. To my surprise, one guard from yesterday's lunch appeared, and he ushered me through the crowd to the gate. Once inside, I thanked him profusely.

"No worries. They've been pretty annoying. I think they're bored right now, so encountering you was a bit like throwing chum into a shark tank," he said with a laugh.

I tried to smile, but the media mob had shaken me a bit. I hoped there would not be footage of me biking awfully on the national news. I hated to think what would happen if Greyson caught sight of that.

The guard helped me find a place for my bike and locate Orson and the Chronos Channel crew. They were off to the far side of the existing golf course, back where a new course was being constructed. I was taken aback by how large the place was, not realizing they had the room for multiple courses.

Besides the TV crew, there was another small team of people. They had a few pop-up tents and were marking every few paces with small pink flags. I wandered up to a man about my height with a tape measure in one hand and a clipboard in the other.

"What are you doing?" I asked him.

"Getting ready to do some STPs." He didn't look at me but pulled out the tape measurer to measure out about twenty-five feet from where he initially stood.

"I'm sorry—what? What are STPs?" My first thought was the car oil additive brand I got for KG with the same initials.

"Shovel Test Pits. STPs. We're working on the first phase of archaeology here. We're making a grid, and then we'll dig a hole every twenty-five feet or so—see, we marked them with the pink flags—and see if there is anything interesting." As he talked, I looked and noticed that there was, indeed, a grid pattern forming across the grass. He was part of a team of about five people, although I guessed several were interns, judging by their ages.

"What would constitute interesting?"

"Well, it could be anything." He led me over to the closest flag. "First, we have to get down deep enough to go below modern intrusion. We'll use shovels and go down, oh, two feet or so. Maybe more. We'll sift the dirt and see if we find any artifacts. Or if we find any sign of a feature there, like if a building was here."

"Or a book cover?"

He shrugged. "Or a book cover. Here, we'd like to find signs from the colonial period. Maybe they're broken parts of a clay pipe."

"What happens if you find something?"

His face lit up. "Anytime we find something, we'll record it and mark it on this map." He held up the clipboard where the final grid was already drawn out. "And if we find an object that looks promising, then we'll do a more involved investigation of the area. These STPs allow us to cover a large area in a short time without being too invasive."

"Seems like a giant game of Battleship."

He laughed. "Pretty much."

Orson stomped towards me like a bull. "What are you doing here?" I caught my breath. His voice was practically a sneer. "Who told you to come here this morning?"

I double-checked, but sure enough, he was directing his anger towards me, not the archaeologist, who quietly disappeared back to the pop-up tent, leaving me to face the shark myself. I looked around, but the rest of the TV crew were too busy assembling their light stands and video cameras and other equipment to notice his sudden change in demeanor. I motioned towards them and explained, "I'm going to be interviewed about the *Book of Kells*."

"Looking to cash in? Huh? Huh?" He pointed a finger towards me. As he stepped closer, I could smell waves of alcohol reeling off him. "Just another money grubber."

"What? No."

"You tried to get a job with me. With Calverton. Cash in on the *Kells*. You… You… money grubber." I think he tried for a different word but repeated it when he apparently couldn't come up with one. "You should leave!"

I backed off a few steps. I noticed his assistant Ruth looking at me, although for a split moment, I noted the worry that crossed her eyes over Orson. He was incredibly drunk. I hoped he didn't treat her so brutally as well.

I put up my hands in surrender and walked away toward the rest of the TV crew. At least Orson didn't follow. I saddled up to Ashley as she was checking a clipboard. "What's up with him?"

"I'd always heard stories about his drinking," she replied. "Then, just before we came down to Rose Mallow, we all met up at his place in D.C. He didn't answer the door. We tried calling, banging on the door, and everything. Eventually, Ruth came by and let us in with a spare key. He was passed out on his bathroom floor, wearing nothing but a towel. It was icky."

"Yuck."

I couldn't help but wonder if he had been drunk on Friday night. Sure, he seemed completely sober at the press conference, but maybe he sometimes recovered quicker than others? Was it possible that he had forgotten the evening's events? That might explain why he was confused about the details.

"Hey. Hey you...Juney...." Orson made his way over to us. "Didn't I tell you to leave?"

"I told you I'm going to do an interview with the Chronos Channel." I stayed next to Ashley and looked at the others nearby for reassurance. However, my new friends blatantly ignored the exchange and went back to their prep work. I glanced at Ruth, but she slowly shook her head. I had been abandoned. "Okay, okay, I get the picture. I'll go." I turned to the TV crew. "But there is no way you're getting my take on things now."

I walked back toward the bike. Naturally, the rain picked up at the same time. I didn't look forward to biking back in a storm, but obviously, I couldn't stay here. I did something useful with my time and headed to the historical society.

As I pedaled away, I heard a voice call out. "Wait, Juniper!" I glanced over my shoulder. It was Leo Calverton. He ran up next to me, holding a large golf umbrella. "I'm sorry. I heard that Orson kicked you out." He tried extending the umbrella to include me, but I backed out.

"Off *your* property." Hurt feelings sometimes caused me to get sassy.

"Please, let me give you a ride. Anywhere you want."

"I think I better go alone. I need to think some things through."

I didn't want to talk to Leo or anyone else after getting chewed out like that. And it didn't help that we were getting drenched now. I noticed the television crew had scrambled to get their recently put out equipment back inside. The archaeologists were huddling under a single pop-up tent.

"Will you still meet me for dinner? How about tonight?" he asked. I shrugged. Things might be better by then, but I wasn't ready to promise anything. To his credit, Leo didn't push the question further. "You should avoid the press out front. Take the back route through the golf course. It sneaks through the old Baytastic Amusement Park next door."

"You don't own that too?" It was a real question, but the tone came out more sarcastic than Leo probably deserved.

"No, we don't. Not yet, anyway."

My eyes grew enormous. I couldn't tell if he was joking or not. However, the rain began pouring harder, and I needed to go.

"I hope to see you tonight. And the ride offer still stands," he said.

"Thanks." However, I had already made my decision, and my stubborn streak refused to let go. I wasn't really upset with Leo, but I didn't feel like I could give in. All I could do was hope there'd be enough rain to push away some of the summer humidity.

I took his advice and snaked my way through the back to the abandoned park. It was hard to appreciate in the rain, but there were still the remains of roller coasters, carnival booths, and a few animal displays. Even in the storm, I could tell the place wasn't in good shape. Small buildings—maybe for games or food stands—had collapsed. The roller coaster had collapsed halfway. If I had time, I would love to return and explore the place. Azalea and I loved going here each summer. But as the rain turned the pathways into mini mud pits, I knew this would not be the time.

Chapter Twelve

I arrived at the historical society soaking wet. At least I made it safely and with the bike—and myself—in one piece. I found a place for the bike under an awning and shook like a puppy dog to get some of the water off. I don't think it helped much. I was drenched.

Nonetheless, I was determined to make use of the place before it closed again in the afternoon. The historical society was located inside an old brick church. According to a display sign outside, the core of the building had been constructed in the 1600s as St. Columba. That seemed oddly appropriate because Columba founded the abbey at Iona in Scotland—where the *Book of Kells* had possibly been created before being moved to Ireland.

Inside was a single large room with whitewashed walls. The pews had been removed and replaced with displays about the town. There was a tall, vaulted ceiling arcing up to a central point. Several arched windows still had stained glass images of saints displayed. I wasn't sure if one might be St. Columba. Below the windows were long, low file cabinets running the length of two walls. Some windows were modern, and a few had air conditioning units in them, blasting cold air upon my wet skin. I shivered as I walked through. On the far wall, where an altar once would have stood, a marble display of the Ten Commandments was still embedded into the wall.

In the middle of the room was a large tabletop display of the town. It had been constructed in the mid-20th century, so it featured the boardwalk along the Chesapeake Bay and the main stores along the small downtown. There was a row of historic houses that included the Wildflower Inn. The old Baytastic Amusement Park was at one end of town, right next to the

Tidewater Cemetery. The Calverton Golf Course was notably smaller than it had become today.

"Excuse me, do you need help?"

I nearly jumped out of my skin at the voice. I hadn't noticed the older gentleman appear. He stared at my dripping wet self with raised eyebrows, but he said nothing insulting. According to his historical society badge, his name was Harold.

"I'm looking for a history on Rose Mallow. And, I have a list of names." These were the names I had noted while at the Calverton Foundation yesterday. I pulled my list out of my pocket. Not surprisingly, it, too, had become wet and more than a bit smudged. At least some names were still readable.

Harold brightened up considerably upon seeing my list. "Well, yes, we can certainly help you with those. If you're amenable, shall we see about getting you dried up? Then I can show you a few books and our vertical files. You must have gotten caught in that awful downpour. Oh, the joy of summer showers."

I smiled gratefully. "Yes, I certainly would be 'amenable.'"

"Good, good. Wait right here. Or even better—take a seat over there," Harold said as he pointed to a couple of folding chairs in a corner. They were nicer chairs with a bit of plush to them. Soon, he was back with a large blanket and a cup of hot tea in a faded "Bayside is the Best Side" mug. "Take your time to warm up a bit. All I ask is that you keep the tea here and away from the materials and displays."

I nodded, understanding. "Thank you so much." I didn't realize how cold I had become, so the blanket and tea were incredibly welcoming. Part of me wanted to curl up and take a nap. I suspected that might go beyond his hospitality, though.

"So you're looking for these old family names. May I ask why? Are you doing a family history? Or looking at the original founding of the town?" Harold was eager to help. As a reference librarian, I understood that impulse all too well. Each question presented to us was a mini mystery to solve.

"I hope it's not too ridiculous."

"Go on," he said with an encouraging smile.

"But have you heard this whole thing about the missing covers of the *Book of Kells* being in Rose Mallow?"

Harold thought for a moment. He snapped his fingers. "You know what—besides pulling some of these books and names, you might find one other resource helpful." He got up and started wandering the room. I knew that look. It was when a librarian was on the scent of the mystery. He opened a file cabinet and rifled through. "Here we go. Yes, you might find these files interesting too. Much later than the founding families, of course, but this is all about the Kells Society. Let me know if you have questions about it."

"The Kells Society?"

"Part secret society, part social club. Dates back over a hundred years or so." He brought the file over to show me. I noted a lot of clippings and articles about Irish heritage: banquets, parades, scholarship funds, and so on. However, several of the names were like the ones I had seen at the Calverton Foundation. They were more modern sounding, or perhaps they had become Americanized. "I'm going to put it on this table for whenever you're ready." He also returned soon with a few books on the history of Rose Mallow, Southern Maryland, and the Chesapeake Bay.

As much as I wanted to stay curled up in the blanket and take my time sipping the tea, my curiosity yearned to see what was inside the Kells Society file. I put the tea down and took the blanket with me to the table to thumb through the thick file.

I had no idea that the rumor about the missing covers being in Rose Mallow had existed for so long. I had assumed this was a completely new discovery, but decades of clippings showed otherwise. Although based on a cursory scan, people would forget for a generation or two before something reminded them again of their particular heritage. An article from around forty years ago discussed a feud emerging between members of the Kells Society. There were members who wanted to convince the state archaeologist to come out and conduct a full excavation of the proposed site. From the map inset, it looked like the same place as the archaeologists were exploring today. Now it was the Calverton Golf Course, but back then, it was a private family farm.

However, another set of members felt the effort distracted from what they considered being the true point of the Kells Society. All the attention on the lost covers was preposterous to them. They wanted to honor the history and heritage of Rose Mallow. They broke off and founded the historical society I now sat in.

"I take it you were part of the historical society side of things," I said to Harold.

"Not me, no, but my older brother was. Before the 'split,' he was an avid member of the Kells Society. For a long while, he honestly believed that the missing covers were somewhere here," Harold said. "He even took me on a mock treasure hunt for them. It turned out to be nothing, but we had a lot of fun."

Just as Harold described the treasure hunt, I came across an article about the event. Intrigued, I asked Harold for any fire insurance maps of the town. He came back with a few from different time periods. One dated back nearly two hundred years. I again saw that the hunt was in the same place as the golf course. I looked at the area over the centuries. However, a thought kept tugging at my brain. Why was this the location everyone assumed held the covers? If they were, why hadn't they been found yet? If everyone believed the covers were here, then why did Rory want to meet me at the cemetery?

To answer the first question, I switched over to the histories of the town. The first one I checked dated to 1906, when Rose Mallow was at its height as a resort town, primarily accommodating rich families looking to escape the heat of downtown Baltimore. As much as these families brought desperately needed money into the economy, they were despised by the locals for being snobby outsiders.

I read in the book how people from Baltimore "came in like tornadoes each June, bringing an influx of activity that consumed everything in their wake. They constructed enormous homes, parks, and clubs. They never interacted with the 'year-rounders' except to consider them their servants, existing for the beck and call. While Rose Mallow became their summer-time paradise, it was anything else for the people who lived here, who waited patiently for September to return."

I wondered if people around here viewed Nana Z or Azalea and myself that way? Of course, Nana Z had permanently moved here much later and had engrossed herself in the town, participating on every board and club she could.

Finally, I found a section in the history book on the "Rumor of the Ancient Ireland Tome." Intrigued, I read on. "The ó Dubhghaill family, later the O'Doyle family, one of the founders of Rose Mallow, has long claimed that they were the ancient protectors of the *Book of Kells*, the fantastic, illustrated manuscript housed in Trinity College, Dublin. Their prized possession is a family diary that suggests the *Book of Kells* were to be brought to Rose Mallow during the awful Cromwell affair for safekeeping. Although it is agreed that they never made the journey, there is less agreement about the covers of the Books. According to family lore, these covers were more of a shrine for the Catholic opus, made of gold and silver and encrusted with hundreds of valuable stones and jewels. While the rest of the world considers them lost to the centuries, Mr. Thomas O'Doyle has argued that his ancestor Tárlach ó Dubhghaill successfully brought the shrine to Rose Mallow but could not retrieve the rest of the book. While he has never seen his ancestor's bounty, he believes it was buried on the family's homestead." The book then trailed off before telling me where the homestead stood. I remembered having seen the ancestral name in the cemetery. I couldn't remember the exact year he had died, but it had been around the 1680s.

I flipped through the rest until I found a section on family histories. Sure enough, there again was the O'Doyle family history. They had been here since the founding of the town. I also found them in the vertical files, a series of file folders with clippings on different topics.

I next went through city directories for them and the other names. City directories were fantastic records. Hard-bound books, they were like the Yellow Pages before phones, and they went back over 150 years sometimes. Some names I saw remained in Rose Mallow for over a hundred years. These were the families that made the town what it was today. However, I couldn't help wondering about the cemetery.

"Do you have materials on the Tidewater Cemetery?" I asked.

"Of course. But, it's getting to be lunchtime, and we're technically supposed to shut down for the next 90 minutes." Harold spoke with a certain bashfulness. I gathered he didn't want to kick me out, but I had a feeling he might have always been a stickler for the rules. As much as I was getting my research stride going, I certainly didn't want to get him in trouble.

"Oh, please. Don't mind me. I'll come back later."

As I gathered my things, Harold found a corner and pulled out his lunch. He switched on a nearby radio.

"Rory Walsh is a person of interest in the death of Tess O'Doyle." I recognized Detective Gupta's voice. "Anyone with knowledge of his whereabouts is asked to call the police."

"That was Detective Lakshmi Gupta discussing the murder of Tess O'Doyle, who was discovered in Tidewater Cemetery on Friday night," said a reporter. "The authorities are searching for Rory Walsh, who is now listed as a person of interest." The reporter droned on, but I noticed that they never mentioned the *Book of Kells*.

I wondered if Azalea had heard the same report. Maybe I should head back to the inn first to check on her. However, a growl in my stomach suggested I better eat something before attempting another bike ride, especially if the rain hadn't yet let up. All I had eaten this morning were a couple of Azalea's muffins. I headed back over to the Purple Oyster Coffee Shop. Fortunately, it had stopped raining, so at least I wouldn't get soaked again. I still hadn't finished drying out from round one.

Maybe I'd also find out something more about Tess and how she was connected to all of this. That remained very unclear to me. She must have found the O'Doyle diary, but had she been the one to contact Orson? And why involve Rory?

After I got my coffee and a spinach and egg souffle, I turned and searched for an empty seat. The café was fairly full. To my surprise, I caught sight of my shadowy, so-called mafia man again. He was the one who had been arguing with Orson at the Foundation's clubhouse yesterday. He was finishing up something and looked to be collecting what was left of his plate and napkins. Breathing in deeply, I mustered up my courage and headed towards his table.

Of course, as I did so, my new phone rang loudly. Desiree must have been messing with me, because "Pour Some Sugar on Me" played as the ringtone. "Oh darn," I muttered. Being new, I hadn't yet set it to be on vibrate. The people in the café looked around to see me. Several smiled, and a few outright laughed.

With my hands full, I couldn't quite get to my 80s hair-band-loving phone. Undeterred, I made my way through the café and promptly put my items down at the shadowy man's table so I could finally check the phone. He watched me with a silent grin.

After all of that song had played, it turned out that I'd received a text from Whitney. "Granny's ready to talk. Meet us in 10 minutes."

"10 minutes?" I nearly shouted. Shadowy man sat back with his arms crossed but obviously amused at my strangeness. He leaned forward to take another sip of his coffee and waited for whatever I planned to do next. What did I plan to do next?

I voted for texting back to Whitney. "I can't get there for over half an hour." That was optimistic, given my food and bike, currently locked up on the rack outside. We were less than a mile away, but naturally, as I looked outside, the rain had started up again.

"Granny won't appreciate waiting."

I debated looking for a car share service. I didn't know if that was a thing in Rose Mallow. As I studied my phone, the shadowy man, perhaps tired of my antics, cleaned up as if to leave. I decided it was now or never.

"Uh, excuse me," I asked him.

"Yes?" His voice has an accent, but I couldn't place it on a single word.

"I'm Juniper Blume."

"A pleasure to meet you, Ms. Blume. I believe you were at the press conference yesterday?" Irish. His accent was definitely Irish. Oh, of course. The green, white, and orange handkerchief in his pocket that I had spotted on Friday. It was for the flag of Ireland.

"Yes, that was interesting."

"One word for it." Little dimples formed in his cheeks as he smiled.

"My apologies for bothering you, but well, uh, I biked over here."

"Ah, I figured you had walked and got caught in that awful downpour." His gaze landed firmly on my still-wet hair.

"Yeah, I must look a bit of a mess."

He shrugged. In other words, I looked worse than I imagined. I tried to spot my reflection in the café window. I couldn't make myself out, but I guessed I had that drowned rat look. I wondered if that would ever be in fashion.

"Well, I'm sorry to be forward, but if you're on your way out, could I, uh, hitch a ride?"

He laughed. "Hitch a ride? You Americans and your colorful turns of phrase. However, are you not about to eat something?" He gestured towards the souffle and coffee in my hands.

I sighed and wiggled my phone as a way of explanation. "Well, now they're to go."

"Fortunately, you've caught me at a good time. I'd be happy to lend you a hand, Ms. Blume."

We climbed into his black sedan, which I noted was emblazoned with diplomat's plates. I prayed that Keisha's bike would be fine being left at the Purple Oyster. I gave him directions to Whitney's grandmother's house, right next to my sister's inn. "So, what brings you to Rose Mallow, Mr....I'm sorry, I didn't ask your name."

"Please, call me Declan. Declan Byrne. I'm here on behalf of the government of Ireland," he said. "We've been very curious about how realistic Orson Bradford's claims were."

"You knew what he was going to announce?" I continued to carry the coffee and souffle, now tucked into a go bag. I wanted desperately to dive into them, but I didn't think that would go over well. Besides, we didn't have far to go.

"Not precisely. But enough. I work for Trinity College."

My eyes grew wide. "That's amazing. You have the *Book of Kells* there. Seeing it in person last year was incredible."

He smiled modestly. "Indeed. So, I wanted to see this so-called O'Doyle diary and assess its authenticity for myself. To make sure Bradford wasn't just another eejit full of hot air, as you might put it."

We both laughed before I turned serious. "But he doesn't have the diary."

"He most certainly does not. I wasn't not pleased when I discovered that truth. And I don't think the Irish government will be," he replied. I assumed that was the moment I had witnessed at the Calverton Club yesterday. Declan must have absolutely lost his cool on Bradford. As he spoke, we pulled up in front of Whitney's grandmother's house. I still had a minute to spare.

As I climbed out of the car, Declan stopped me to hand me a business card. "I've heard you work with the Library of Congress. I would love to connect—whether about this or anything else." Unfortunately, I didn't have a card with me to return to him, but I graciously accepted his and expressed my appreciation for the ride.

Chapter Thirteen

I made it up to the front steps at exactly the ten-minute mark. When Whitney opened the door, she looked glum that I had made it there in time. However, that defeated expression soon passed as she surveyed my wet mess. Plus, I continued to carry my coffee and souffle.

"Did you bring a present?" she asked, nodding towards the items in my hand.

"You caught me as I was about to have lunch," I answered truthfully.

"Looks more like I caught you in the middle of a shower." She stepped aside and led me in. There was a large mirror in the house's foyer. I caught sight of myself and gasped. My hair was a dried, frizzy mess, my makeup had run, and my face was blotchy. Not to mention that my shoes were still wet and squeaked as I walked across the marble floor. "I certainly can't believe that Miss Perfect would ever allow herself to go out in public like *that.*"

I bit back a return insult and simply nodded. "It's not my best look."

"Have you heard anything about Rory?" she asked. I shook my head no. "Too bad. So strange that he disappeared just as he had been finally set free."

"Set free?"

"You know, because of the divorce." She waved a hand as if what she had said was obvious. "He and your sister had been together for eons. So the timing struck me as ironic."

"I guess so," I replied. "Wait, did you still have a crush on him?"

"I'm not a teenager anymore. I have a boyfriend, remember? Back in Annapolis?" I noticed that Whitney's voice had gone up. I wanted to laugh. As a teen, her feelings for Rory had been painfully obvious, but he was only interested in Azalea.

"Oh, right, at the Naval Academy."

"Some of us aren't caught up in the past."

A screech like a dying barn owl greeted me. Cordelia Sullivan came into the foyer and spotted my wet ensemble. "You came here looking like a drowned cat? Did you honestly believe this was acceptable?"

"Granny, Juniper is trying." Whitney tried defending me. I was touched. However, her effort was interrupted by her grandmother.

"Whitney Sullivan. You are no prize yourself this afternoon. It's as if you forgot I wanted to see you." She wandered over and began adjusting parts of her granddaughter's outfit. "Now, stand up straighter. Straighter. Taller. And stop wearing so much makeup. Makes you look like a streetwalker."

I was horrified. Whitney quietly accepted her grandmother's harshness, although I could see tears forming in the back of her eyes.

"Look, I should go," I said and backed up to the door. A beaten-down Whitney offered to walk out. We had barely made it into the house, to begin with. Cordelia said nothing but watched us with disgust, as if we were rats in her kitchen.

"I'm sorry, Juniper. I really want to help," she said. "I've known Rory since he was in diapers—well, I was too, and as much as he could be annoying, I don't believe he hurt Tess."

"Thank you. I had wanted to ask about some of the founding families and the Kells Society."

"The Kells Society?" Cordelia repeated. I hadn't realized she'd kept up with us. I turned to her. Her thin, drawn-on eyebrows had popped up, intruding up into her forehead. "Why, I was the last Queen of the Kells."

To my shock, her face and posture relaxed, and she spoke with genuine enthusiasm. As she talked, she wandered over to the parlor. Whitney and I looked at each other and silently followed Cordelia. She led us to the large, ornate fireplace mantel where a few framed black and white photos stood. One showed off a large group of young adults, probably in their twenties, each with a large shamrock on their lapels. They had their arms draped around each other while sitting atop the boardwalk railing and flashed enormous smiles for the camera.

Another photo featured a starlet with a tiara covered in large shamrocks. It took me a second glance to realize that was Cordelia as a young woman. Her hair must have been golden, as it was bright white in the photo. She sported a cape that closed with a Celtic knot-style brooch. She was absolutely stunning. Next to her was a young man I didn't recognize with a similar cape and a shamrock-styled crown. While she gazed straight at the camera, his look never left her.

"Now, the Kells Society, they were the true keepers of Rose Mallow's heritage. Except for when they'd get caught up in these silly endeavors to find the eponymous books. Hah. Well, it was all in good fun. Except for when Bobby O'Doyle announced he knew where they were."

"Bobby O'Doyle?" I repeated, thinking of Harmony and Tess O'Doyle. Cordelia nodded toward the photo of her with the young man.

"Oh, he was a looker, that Bobby." She sighed audibly, and her eyelashes fluttered, as if she was remembering some Hollywood heartthrob. She sat down on an extremely rigid sofa that didn't seem to adjust under her weight.

"Granny," Whitney said, looking mortified at her grandmother's admission.

"Well, he was. You might have been an O'Doyle, young lady, if things had gone a bit differently." We were both stunned by that revelation. I turned back to the photograph, but Whitney nearly knocked me over, trying to get a closer look at him. I didn't fight her on it.

Cordelia laughed at our efforts. "Oh, come now, Whitney. I had already married your grandfather by that point. And Bobby had married Janet Keller. They had a little girl and another on the way. It was too late for anything." She squeezed her eyes shut and shook her head, reminding me of a small child trying to refuse to take her medicine. I had the impression that Cordelia Sullivan wasn't prone to playing "What Might Have Been?" if she could help it.

"Anyway, it was 1963 when Bobby announced he knew where the book and cover were. Claimed their location was a long-held family secret. Everyone laughed, but he got red-faced serious. He said he was going to be a millionaire." Cordelia got a far-away look on her face. Her gaze drifted towards the back of the house.

"What happened?" Whitney beat me to the question.

She snapped out of her reverie. "Of course, he didn't know where they were. Such a silly, misguided attempt at what, I don't know, adventure, perhaps?"

"Do you know where he looked for them?" I asked.

She stood up slowly, having to use the couch arm for help. Whitney tried to help, but she pushed her aside. She walked over to a framed map of Rose Mallow and tapped out on the water. The spot was miles away from where the current excavation was happening. I wondered what led him to that area.

"They found his body a few days later. He had drowned in the Chesapeake Bay."

"Oh, my," I said.

Cordelia shook her head. Her look seemed a mixture of sadness, pity, and utter disappointment. I wondered how deeply her feelings had run for him. Whitney joined her grandmother by the picture. Cordelia slightly flinched when Whitney placed a hand on her shoulder.

"No one believed him or wanted to join on his mission. But Bobby was stubborn. He went out by himself on his father's boat. I think he thought he'd be a hero. Or that he'd be a millionaire. Such foolishness." She sucked her lips and tsked a few times. Then she shoved off Whitney's touch and headed back to the sofa.

"Is that what ended the Kells Society?" I asked.

"Mostly. There had always been disagreements. I stayed with the group interested in forming the historical society. That poor family. And now Bobby's grandniece is dead, too." Cordelia shook her head. There was a long, awkward silence before she finally said, "I'm sorry. I think I need to lie down for a bit. Whitney, would you kindly see our guest out?" She suddenly looked so much older and smaller, much less the regal matron of society who had initially dismissed my inquiry. It was disconcerting to watch.

The about-face of her mood puzzled me, but I don't think it was surprising to Whitney. She simply nodded and walked me to the door. I wanted to ask about the family tree she had mentioned, but I didn't want to intrude further.

Instead, I expressed my appreciation to Whitney for having me over.

I walked onto the porch and waited for the rain to stop before running next door to the Wildflower Inn. As I stood there, I heard Whitney with her grandmother, realizing a window was open behind me.

"You never should have brought her here," Granny said. I assumed they were talking about me.

"I had to, Granny. She hounded me."

I wouldn't have called it hounding, but I wasn't going to split hairs.

"She's a smart one. She's going to figure it all out." I wondered what that meant, but I guessed it had to do with the *Book of Kells*. Maybe Granny knew something more than she had told me?

"No, she won't, Granny. I promise." Whitney's voice sounded desperate.

"You've been clumsy." Granny tsked her teeth. "You need to be more careful. Not very becoming of a Sullivan."

"Granny, you don't know the stress I've been under. I've been very careful."

Then suddenly, the window slammed shut. Whitney stared at me through the glass. I gave a sheepish wave. She pulled the curtains closed.

The rain had finally stopped. After popping over next door to the inn to give Clover a quick walk, I headed back to the Purple Oyster to retrieve Keisha's bike. I then biked over to the Tidewater Cemetery to join the search party for Rory. There was a large group of people, probably over a hundred. I was extremely touched by this show from the town. All weekend, I had heard references to rumors about Rory being involved with Tess's murder, so I appreciated people were putting aside that unsubstantiated claim and had come here to find him. It was also a testament to Desiree, Keisha, and the others for organizing this event so quickly, but I think we all understood how time was of the essence.

The group was forming lines and getting organized to start the search under the direction of the local police. I didn't spot Detective Gupta, but I saw Deputy Torres hanging out with a few other members of the police department. He spotted me and locked on with his stare, not bothering to nod. I felt cold, even in the heat, and shivered. Finally, I broke free from his gaze and turned away.

To my surprise, Harmony was there, too, although she kept her head low, avoided eye contact, and looked more frazzled than usual.

Interestingly, I also spotted Whitney. I wondered if she had left not long after me, perhaps while her grandmother was napping. She waved at me. "I couldn't miss a chance to help. I'm glad they organized this," she said.

"I'm glad you came," I said earnestly.

I knew Azalea was still at the inn, which was good. I didn't want her to be the one to potentially find, well, anything really. Besides, she had Vi to manage and a whole TV crew to babysit.

I joined up with Keisha and Desiree. They showed me a map of the cemetery, on which a grid had been superimposed. We spent the afternoon walking slowly in our small groups, covering a designated area of the grid. The work was tedious. Being June after a storm, the weather sat upon us like a heavy blanket, nearly smothering with its humidity. Still, we continued, walking slowly out towards the edge, which was ringed with a thick band of trees. I saw police dogs going into the forest to put their super sniffers to work. I alternated between hoping they would and wouldn't find anything.

In the end, no one found any trace of Rory. I didn't know if this was good or bad news. Everyone was exhausted and drenched from the heat. I was no longer alone in my wet cat style, but that small joke didn't make me feel much better.

"Wait, wait, there's something over here!"

I didn't see who spoke, but soon, there was a group of people running over to the far end of the cemetery. I joined them, and we caught up to a small circle of others. In the center was Whitney. She held up a waterlogged book—a very old book with a damaged leather cover.

I gasped. Could it be? Had she found the missing O'Doyle diary? I pushed ungenerously through the crowd. She caught sight of me and held up the book towards me.

"Is this the diary?" Whitney asked.

"I don't know." I caught up with her and gently took the book from her hands. The binding was old, and the leather was cracked. The pages were in

128

horrible shape, likely from spending the weekend in the cemetery. Honestly, I wasn't sure if the book was salvageable.

However, before I could peek inside, Deputy Torres appeared and whisked the book out of my hands. I protested, but he gave me such a death stare that I backed down. The police bagged it up for evidence and flagged the spot where it had been found.

"Can I spend more time looking at it?" I asked.

He looked at me as if I was ridiculous for asking. "No, it's evidence."

"But it's the only way we'll know if they really are the missing covers for the *Book of Kells*," I replied.

"Great. Then, hopefully, it'll be important evidence." He walked away from me, and I was left wondering if I would ever see inside. If it wasn't the O'Doyle diary, then what was it? And if it was the diary, it was going to need a conservator to help preserve it before it deteriorated further. After all that rain and moisture, I imagined it'd be best going into a freezer. It's what we recommend for emergency salvage of wet leather books. In fact, it'd be best going into a deep freezer with a frost-free setting, allowing the book to dry out slowly. I needed to let Detective Gupta know before they inadvertently destroyed the "important evidence."

I called her, and she picked up on the first ring. "They found the O'Doyle diary. I think."

"No kidding. Where's it now?"

I walked around the edge of the cemetery. The rest of the search team disbanded, and people headed home. A few stragglers still lingered, chatting.

"They bagged it up for evidence. But it needs special care. It's very old and soaked." I launched into a quick lesson about caring for books that have been soaked. Detective Gupta listened without interruption. I thought I heard her scratching notes, but I couldn't be certain.

"Okay, I'll be in touch with them. We'll get it figured out."

"I'm relieved to hear you say that." This was true. I believed she would take it seriously and for that, I was grateful.

"As soon as we get off the phone, I'm going to check in about the O'Doyle diary. Glad to hear it's likely been recovered. I've been getting phone calls all weekend from whack-a-doodles who claim they've found the covers. The first time or two, I admit we took it seriously, but now I know better," she said with a laugh. I think she sounded more amused than irritated. "I had thought southern Maryland would be quieter than when I worked in Baltimore, but it's just, uh, different."

"Yeah, same with D.C.," I replied.

"Look, since you're an expert in rare books, can you stop by tomorrow? I want you to look at this book. I'd like your opinion on it."

Today was already Monday. How much longer could I get away with not being at work? It wasn't like I had requested any time off to be here. I hadn't told anyone I was going, and I was ignoring Greyson's manic texts. But my sister needed me. My car was messed up. I was lucky to now have a working phone. I would have to explain later in the week what had happened. Consequences would be whatever they would be.

"Yes, I'll be happy to help however I can," I replied.

"Good, good. Now I hear you've had some troubles with your car?"

I remained worried about KG and how she was going to fare from her brush with vandalism. "Yeah, that was something to discover."

"Let me ask you something. I've heard about these so-called 'trinkets' being left at your sister's place. Do you think it could be related? That it could be the same person?" The detective's question surprised me. I hadn't expected her to seek my advice. On an old book, I understood, sure, but not on a question like this. I wondered why she was asking me.

"You don't think those were left by Rory?" I asked.

"I don't know. I'll explore every angle, though," she replied.

I considered that. "Azalea has been getting the crushed flowers and messages left for a while now, but she never had her minivan tampered with. At least not that I am aware of."

"So you think the car damage was meant for you specifically?"

I didn't like the sound of that statement. "That's what I think."

Then, a thought pierced through me. What if it was the same person? Who wasn't Rory? What if it was an escalation? But who would do this and why? I was gathering more questions but ending up with fewer answers.

"Even if this hadn't happened, I'd rather you back off things. People have noticed that you're asking questions and exploring angles. I understand the impulse, Juniper, but it's not a smart idea," she said.

"I understand, but—"

"No buts. I know you want to help, but leave it to us. Okay?" With that, Detective Gupta hung up on me. For a moment, I thought she was pulling me into the case and taking my word as an expert, but then to be told like a small child to stay out of things.

There were still a few people hanging around the cemetery. The deputies finished up, and I saw Torres staring at me again. I tried to ignore him. He just wanted what was best for Azalea, I tried to remind myself.

Keisha and Desiree offered to give me a ride, but I gestured towards the bike. It was amazing that it—and I—were still in one piece. Sure, the bike had become dirty, but at least it worked. Keisha felt slightly different.

"What have you done to her?" Her voice was almost a moan. She ran over to the bike and examined it.

"What do you mean?"

"She's...she's...." Keisha stopped talking and threw her hands up in the air.

"Is Keisha okay?" I asked Desiree.

"Depends on how you define okay?" she said with a laugh. "But really, she'll be alright. She takes her bike seriously. How about this? Keisha, you ride the bike back to the inn, and Juniper, you ride with me?"

Keisha wasn't listening. She petted the bike like you might a horse. I saw her whispering something to it. Oh, teenagers.

Chapter Fourteen

When I got back to the inn, Azalea was at the front desk. I caught her up about the search and Whitney finding the O'Doyle diary. As we talked, Vi played with Clover across the carpet in the foyer. My sister smiled weakly. "Vi has become really attached to him."

"He has a way of snuggling into people's hearts." I sat down next to them, hugged Vi, and then gave Clover a few pets. He rolled over, and I rewarded him with some vigorous belly rubs. "He's a great dog."

"He is, indeed. I almost want to change our pet policies, but I don't know that everyone would have a pet as friendly and warm as Clover." He heard Azalea say his name and perked up. She laughed. "Sorry, Clover, nothing for you to eat right now." He cocked his head to the side as she talked.

Vi kept repeating, "Clov-ah. Good puppy, Clov-ah." He gave her a few generous licks on her face.

"You think that after his, uh, mess yesterday?" I asked, thinking about his slip-up in the library when Detective Gupta was here.

She shook her head but smiled. "Yep, even with that. I mean, I have a three-year-old, and messes happen. Frequently. And what should I do? Ban babies? Never." She came around and joined us, sitting on the rug. I wondered what would happen if any of the Chronos TV crew arrived now and saw us hanging out here. We must have made for a truly professional sight.

"How long is the TV crew staying?" I asked, having thought about them.

"At least through tomorrow. What I've gathered is that if they find anything amazing, then they may stay longer. I don't have anyone else coming in until

132

next Friday, so I've told them it isn't a problem. Otherwise, they're on to whatever is their next mission on Monday."

"Must be quite the life. Traveling around to film all these things," I said with a touch of envy. I had spent a year after college traveling the globe. Finally, I settled down and got my library degree, figuring I could continue my love of travel vicariously through books. While it hadn't fully managed my craving for travel, it had at least quieted the call. Anytime I needed a travel fix, I played a game. I wandered the halls at the Library of Congress and stopped at a random shelf, picking up whatever book was there. It could be anything from an obscure research tome on some mathematical treatise to *Gone with the Wind*. Either way, I gave myself a few minutes to disappear as fully as I could into the book's new world. At least until Greyson yelled at me for being behind.

"I guess so. But I'd rather be here with my quiet life. Well, normally quiet." As she spoke, Vi got up and chased Clover around the room. The little dog happily engaged, barking the whole time. It was delightfully controlled chaos. I saw why Azalea enjoyed being here. I had brushed off the idea of staying in one place, but Rose Mallow was charming and precious, and if I could get past my hurt, it was still a piece of our grandmother. Above Vi and Clover was another one of Nana Z's paintings, this one of the Chesapeake Bay at dusk.

"I'm sorry I've disturbed that peace and quiet for you." I'd felt that way ever since Deputy Torres had accused me yesterday of adding to Azalea's stress instead of alleviating it. I hated to admit it, but he had been right. Even if nothing else had happened, I had been thoughtless by swooping in to stay here out of the blue while planning to meet with her soon-to-be ex-husband. They were selfish actions, and I was sorry for not considering the consequences.

"I'm glad you're here. Really," she replied and placed a hand upon mine. "I've missed you." She sighed. "I guess I should ask how things went during the search party. I'm not sure I want to know, but then again, no one has called or shown up at my door yet, so I figured..." Her voice broke.

"Hey, hey, it's all right. We didn't find him. But the diary at the center of this all may have been located. It's pretty damaged after being in the hot cemetery and then the rain, but it might be salvageable."

"I don't care about any ancient book. Except, why? Why was Rory involved with it?"

"I don't know for sure. The diary belonged to Tess's family. That's why it was called the O'Doyle diary." I debated telling Azalea about how Tess's grandfather Bobby—Harmony's father—had drowned searching for the same covers decades ago. I didn't think it would help anything. Besides, it didn't answer the question of why Rory was the one to call me about the O'Doyle diary. There was a thought at the back of my head that had formed, but it wasn't fully fleshed out yet. I needed to do more research first.

I glanced down at my watch. "Oh, shoot. I need to go."

"You just got back. Where are you going?"

"I need to shower and dress. I'm going to dinner with Leo Calverton," I replied.

To my surprise, Azalea's entire demeanor swiftly shifted. "You're doing what? Dinner with that swindler?" She stood upright with her hands firmly on her hips. Her face soured into a look of utter disgust.

"Uh, yes?"

"I can't believe you. You come waltzing in here, at the center of all this mess, and then you add to it by going on a date—a date!—with one of the most despicable families in Rose Mallow?" Azalea got up and practically stomped her way back over to the registration desk. Fortunately, Vi and Clover hadn't noticed her mood change and continued playing their game of tag and chase through the downstairs of the house.

"I don't understand. What is so horrible about Leo?"

She looked at me curiously, almost as if she were sniffing out if I was telling the truth. "You don't know, do you?"

Obviously, I didn't, but I shook my head furiously.

She sighed loudly and relaxed slightly. "I'm sorry, but your date's family wants to develop Rose Mallow. They want to turn this place into the same thing as over at National Harbor."

"You mean the mega development with the big hotels and casino? And the

Ferris wheel?" I enjoyed going to National Harbor. There were some nice restaurants and shops there. The place had been created out of seemingly thin air along the Potomac River, just south of D.C. Now, it was a major tourist attraction. What I had never considered was what the residents in the area thought of all that being plopped down into their neighborhood. I didn't know if they liked National Harbor or hated it.

"Yep. Make Rose Mallow the hottest spot on the Chesapeake." She searched the front desk until she found a brochure. She pushed it towards me. "See, look at this."

I thumbed through the brochure. It showcased a very different Rose Mallow, which had been renamed on the pamphlet to become "Chesapeake Port, a Luxury Waterfront Experience."

I read aloud, "Only an hour south of D.C. and Baltimore, but a million miles from it all. Enjoy the charm of the Chesapeake with signature shops and celebrity chefs." There was no longer the historic character of my sister's Wildflower Inn or the eclectic charm of the Purple Oyster coffee shop. Instead, the boardwalk looked like a mini–New York skyline with tall towers, neon signs, chain restaurants, and a mega casino. There were tremendous crowds. It was overkill for such a small community.

Instead of a Ferris wheel, the Baytastic Amusement Park had been rebranded as an "adventure experience" and moved to literally hang over the water. They wanted to turn the Chesapeake Bay into a colossal water park. A huge roller coaster went out over the water while another ride apparently dumped people into the water itself. The idea that Rose Mallow would become some sort of Vegas on the Bay was disturbing.

Now I understood why Leo didn't venture into town very often. The people who lived and worked here must have hated this plan. It practically demolished all of Rose Mallow with a steamroller and reconstructed it into a getaway for the rich and famous.

"Where did you get this?" I asked.

"Representatives for the Calvertons passed this out at the last Chamber of Commerce meeting. They did this whole big presentation about it, too. Several people walked out. I stayed and tried to ask questions with a few others, but they didn't want to listen to us. They gave rehearsed answers or talked right over me, waving away our concerns. It was infuriating." As she talked, she hit the front desk to punctuate her frustration. I worried about the wood more than my sister's hand.

"Is there a plan to counteract their efforts?"

"Yes. No. Maybe. There are several plans, really, but none that everyone is behind yet. It's going to be a fight, but if we don't get our act together, then it'll be all over before we can even take our first swing," she replied. In contrast to her fury, Vi and Clover ran back into the room and around my legs, nearly knocking me over. I hoped it was getting some good energy out of both of them. I wasn't sure how good of a sleeper Vi was, but fortunately for me, Clover slept hard—once he eventually went down.

"Do you want me to cancel my date?" I wasn't sure I wanted to go on it anymore myself.

"No. Yes. Maybe." Azalea repeated. She sat down and put her head in her hands. "You should go. One date with the devil will not make or break anything."

"Maybe I can find out more information about their plans?" I wiggled my fingers in front of my face, trying to look devious.

"It's not like they're hiding them, though. But yeah, it wouldn't hurt to have an insider. "

There was also a curiosity building inside of me. Maybe the date could be more of an undercover operation than anything romantic. I pictured myself being Rose Mallow's secret champion and getting the Calverton family to change their minds. It was a foolish fantasy, but it gave me a smile.

"I'm really glad you're here," she said.

"I'm sorry it's taken me so long. And I'm sorry for how things have gone so far," I said and came back behind the desk to wrap her in a hug.

"You want to know a secret?" she asked.

"Always."

"I'm glad you didn't come sooner," she said. I pulled back, not expecting her to say that. "It's not that I didn't want you here, but I don't think I could have handled it. After Nana Z died, I was devastated. I put everything I had into the Wildflower Inn. It consumed me. That and, of course, Violet. I didn't want to do anything but work on this building and take care of my baby. I don't think I could have handled you being here too, because you remind me so much of Nana Z. And I knew you were grieving in your own way. I don't think I could have handled more grief, at least not then. I know that's selfish."

"I get it. Truly, I do. We would have pulled each other more down than up," I said.

She nodded. "Yeah, exactly. You know, I think that's when Rory and I fell apart. I was so consumed by my grief, and then that was compounded by having a new baby. I was overwhelmed and threw myself completely into these projects. I essentially abandoned him. And I don't think he knew what to do for me. We hung on, but by the time the worst of it had passed, we had both changed."

I hugged her deeply. "Oh, Azalea. I'm so sorry. That must have been horrible."

She shrugged. "It was, but it's past. Or it was. All of this about Rory missing and Tess's death is making it hard to hold on to the person I had finally become."

"You're a strong person, Azalea. Hands down the strongest person I know," I said.

"Thanks," she replied and melted into my arms. However, after a moment, she jumped back up and said, "Oh no. You better get ready. You need to get going soon, don't you?"

"Don't worry about it," I replied, but I still let go. She was right. I barely had enough time to pop into the shower and make myself presentable. I raced over to the Carriage House and waddled my way through the box towers to the bathroom. I don't think I had ever pulled myself together in such record time. When I came out, Azalea was in the Carriage House's main room with Violet and Clover. She held a garment bag in her arms.

"I wasn't sure if you had anything, well, uh, nice? You know, to wear for your date. So, I pulled this out. It belonged to Nana Z. It's a bit long on me, but I thought it might work for you."

She held up the most spectacular dress I had ever seen. It was a vintage Dior "New Look" dress with a crepe-de-chine silk and a blue and gold floral pattern. The dress featured an oversized portrait collar that crossed over the bodice. Buttons covered with the same fabric cascaded below the collar to the full, pleated skirt. I was astounded. I had never seen a dress so exquisite.

"Pretty," Violet said.

"You...." I stumbled over the words. Azalea laughed. She held out the dress and a crinoline. She even had a pair of nude heels. I tried again to thank her, but my throat was literally dry.

"Put it on," she said.

I took the dress back with me and put it on as quickly as I could safely manage, afraid I'd rip or tear this treasure. It fit like a glove. Azalea and Violet "oohed" and "aahed" as I came out. She helped me pin up my hair, fix my makeup, and added one of Nana Z's pearl necklaces as the final touch. Clover raced around us as we worked. Vi helped, handing us pieces from Nana Z's jewelry box.

"You look just like her," she said with tears in her eyes. I found a longer mirror and was shocked to see how much I looked like 1950s photos of when Zinnia had been our age. We could have been twins. Really, triplets with Azalea. It was astounding. I had to blink back my own tears. I would not ruin how much I looked like Nana Z with a cry right now.

"Thank you, Azalea. This is absolutely incredible." At least this time, I got the words out. Clover sat at my feet and looked up at me. He cocked his head to the side and barked once in what I took as appreciation.

"I have one more surprise for you," she said. I didn't deserve additional surprises. I didn't deserve any of this. She led me out to the wraparound porch in front of the inn. "Earlier today, when I was cleaning everything, I cleaned your car."

"KG?"

I didn't wait for her to answer. I ran out to the street, where my car waited underneath a cover. I ripped it off and nearly fell to my knees. My vintage roadster looked brand new. There were no signs that she had been vandalized.

"How did you get it off?"

"It washed off easily," she said with a shrug. "I don't know what they used, but it wasn't painted. Maybe foam? But it looked worse than it was."

"And the tires? They're fixed!"

"The car dealership where Rory works wanted to do something to help, so they jumped at the chance," she said.

"Oh, thank goodness." I hugged my car. Clover ran over and joined me. He tried to jump inside. Of course, it was just as I had my arms wrapped around my car that Leo Calverton pulled up in his brand-new black Tesla.

"Well, that's not something you see every day," he said as he climbed out. He carried flowers in his arms. They were a beautiful summer bouquet of sunflowers, daisies, blue delphinium, and purple hydrangeas. "I guess I don't give my cars enough appreciation. Although, is that a Karmann Ghia?" He waltzed over and ran his hand over KG's driver-side front door. "Wow. You don't see those very often. Perhaps we should take this instead."

I stood up. He stopped talking as soon as he caught sight of me. Then, he said, "Wow, Juniper. I didn't think you could look any lovelier, but you are amazing."

"Thanks. I've been told I clean up all right."

"Better than all right." He handed me the flowers. They were gorgeous. Definitely not your ready-made corner store bouquet.

From the porch, Azalea called out, "Come back in, Violet and Clover. We'll get you some dinner." As much as Clover loved riding in KG, he loved food more. He happily abandoned me and raced back inside. Where he went, Violet stumbled after.

"I mean it," he said. "We should go in your car."

"Okay, but I'm the only one who gets to drive KG."

"KG? Oh, for Karmann Ghia. Sure, sure. Happy to be chauffeured around. We don't have far to go. I made reservations at the Indigo Room at the end of the boardwalk," he said. We climbed in, and I handed the flowers back to him. It was a lovely night, so I dropped KG's top and prayed my pinned and pomaded hair would stay relatively in place. I wished I had found a driving scarf to sport. I may have driven slower than usual.

As we drove to the restaurant, we got a few gawking stares from people on the street. I wanted to believe it was because of KG or my vintage ensemble, but I strongly suspected that it was because of me. "People must have learned that I was the one who found Tess," I said to him as I parked near the boardwalk.

Leo shook his head. "Unfortunately, this happens anytime I go anywhere in Rose Mallow. It's difficult when your family is like mine."

I wanted to ask him more, but we had reached the restaurant. The inside of the Indigo Room had deeply blue walls that matched its name. The tables were covered in white cloth, and the chairs were black and silver. A long wall of windows looked out over the Chesapeake Bay. A waiter led us out to a table on the terrace with a large white and blue paisley-patterned umbrella overhead. A clear vase with fresh flowers sat in the middle of the table. The view was spectacular.

For a Monday night, there were a surprising number of people in the restaurant. As with the outside, there were definitive murmurs as we walked through. I still wasn't sure I believed it was all because of Leo. Instead, I tried to focus my attention on the menu.

"Being a vegetarian, I thought it might be hard to find something, but I'm impressed with how many choices they have here," I said.

Leo laughed lightly. "If you think being a vegetarian is difficult, try being a gluten-intolerant vegan. I basically live on salads. And those can be tiring. What I wouldn't give for a really good pizza sometimes, but please, don't tell anyone."

I smiled. He made a gesture, putting his hand out to meet mine, but I pulled it back. I wasn't ready for that. My sister's revelation about "Chesapeake Port" still danced through my memory.

"Azalea showed me the...." I started to say, but we were interrupted by the waiter. We placed our orders. Leo ordered an expensive bottle of wine.

"You were saying?" he prompted me after the waiter left.

"Azalea showed me the brochure. The one about Port Chesapeake or something like that."

He slumped a bit in his seat, but nodded. "Chesapeake Port. *The* Luxury

Waterfront Experience." He enunciated each word, making them sound like they were each capitalized. "It's my brother's pet project. You remember Cecil, right?"

Unfortunately, I couldn't forget running into Cecil and Elsa in the storage room at the Calverton Foundation. I also couldn't control the shudder or pursing my lips. Leo laughed.

"The board loves the concept. Probably because they're either family members who turn up their noses at the locals or out-of-towners without any personal connections to Rose Mallow. My brother is trying so hard to make a name for himself in the family." Leo gave a bitter laugh. "He doesn't realize it doesn't matter. Nothing you do is ever good enough for them."

"What do you think about it?"

"The development project? Oh, I think it's a horrific idea. I've tried proposing we capitalize on the quaint charm of Rose Mallow and invest in the local community, but the board is completely against it. They want to rebuild the area in their own image." He pointed across the water. "Over there is St. Michael's. They have unique restaurants, boutiques, a luxury hotel, and a great museum. Have you ever been to their Sea Glass festival? Fantastic. And all of that is building on their existing strengths. Rose Mallow could easily do that."

I had been to St. Michael's before a few times. It was the very definition of the word "charming." However, so was Rose Mallow. "We have unique restaurants and boutiques, and this great boardwalk. Plus, our neighborhood of historic houses. Imagine if someone updated Baytastic. That could pull people here."

"Right, exactly." A fire lit in Leo's eyes. He leaned across the table towards me. "Build on our strengths. Rose Mallow has many. I just need to convince the board to see the same thing." As we chatted, our food arrived. Leo poured me a glass of the best pinot grigio I had ever tasted. "See, this wine? It came from a local winery. We have great wineries in the area, too. And they're opening a distillery nearby as well."

"But the board wants what? Las Vegas on the Bay?"

"Yeah, essentially." He smiled. "It's nice having someone to talk to about this. Everyone in my family is so excited about this project. I mean, they'll find fault with it and him soon, and there will be in-fighting over the details, but for right now, I'm the black sheep for not wanting to take it on."

"So, what are you excited about?" I asked, leaning in closer on the table.

"I was raised to be a developer, but as I told you in the storage room, that's not my passion. I was telling the truth, though. The collections really interest me. I've been watching what's happening with Glenstone up in Potomac," he said. I nodded, having recently visited the new private museum with its modern art collection and acres of land, being filled with art installations. It was a fascinating place. It reminded me of how many museums in D.C. started out in the same way, being private collections that the owners wanted to share with the public. Everywhere from the Phillips Collection, Hillwood Estate, the Kreiger, and the Corcoran had started that way.

"You want to turn the collections into a museum? About colonial Maryland?"

"Really, about the creation of America. Maybe expand beyond that. I have some ideas, not fully fleshed out. You saw the tip of the iceberg. We have a remarkable collection, and I don't want it to stay locked away forever." His voice rippled with passion. I understood. That's why I worked at the Library of Congress. Being able to share the treasures of our culture with the world was important to me.

He leaned closer across the table. I leaned towards him until our faces were inches from each other. "Can I tell you a secret?"

"Of course."

He looked back and forth. "I can't run the museum."

"Why is that?"

"Because I've decided that whether we find the covers to the *Book of Kells* or not, I'm going to keep trying. I will not let worrying about what my family thinks of me stand in my way. I'm going to return some lost treasure to the world," he said with a conviction that struck me as highly attractive.

"Will the museum exist to, what, show off your finds?" As much as I liked the idea of recovering lost cultural artifacts, I wasn't too keen on bringing them back to Rose Mallow. If he ever found Alaric's Roman gold, I believed it should be given to Italy, not hoarding them here in Maryland. If we found the *Book of Kells'* covers, I felt like they should be returned to Ireland.

"No. Maybe have an exhibit about them, but I want the museum to focus on my family's collection. I don't know. Maybe the research aspect could be part of the museum somehow. Like I said, I don't have the idea fleshed out yet."

"The birth of a museum. That's pretty exciting," I said.

As we talked, the waiter brought out our meal. I may have devoured my mushroom risotto in less than four minutes. Probably not the most romantic way to eat, but not only was I apparently starving, the dish was decadent and delicious. I don't think I could have stopped, even if I had wanted to. Part of me had to hold back on ordering a second helping.

Leo enjoyed a curry with sweet potatoes, lentils, and Swiss chard. While I had downed my dinner too quickly to share, he was kind enough to offer me a taste. It was fantastic. Everything was brimming with flavor.

"Incredible!" I said.

"It really is."

"Leo, can I ask you something?" I decided it was past time to find out if he was the man I had seen go after Tess on Friday night. He hadn't brought it up, so I wondered if I had been mistaken.

"Of course, anything."

"Well...."

Suddenly, Harmony O'Doyle came stomping across the restaurant, practically thundering at us, "Leonard Calverton! How dare you show your face here!"

I started to say something, but Leo put his hand on top of mine and shook his head. "Harmony O'Doyle. It's good to see you."

"But not to see you. How dare you? If you don't leave in the next thirty seconds, I'm going to call the police." Her face was ablaze with fury.

"Come now, Harmony."

"Don't you 'Harmony' me! After what you did to Tess, you have some nerve."

"What do you think he did to Tess?" I asked.

"I didn't do anything to Tess," replied Leo.

"Liar! I know you were taking her away from me!" Harmony pointed a finger into Leo's chest. He looked annoyed but didn't move her hand.

"I did no such thing."

"All you Calvertons are the same. You think you own us little people. Just like you thought you could own Tess."

"What are you talking about?" I asked.

Harmony swiveled to face me. "Your boyfriend here is a rotten, two-faced weasel. He filled my girl's head with false dreams and floated money in front of her if she'd run away."

"I did no such thing." He repeated his line with more intensity. Leo's face was red, and he was obviously struggling not to yell.

Harmony ignored him and kept her eyes locked on me. "Now I wish that's all he did. If she had run away, then she could run back, you know? But she can never come back now." She dropped her face and sobbed. I stood up and walked over to her, tentatively placing a hand on her shoulder and patting it.

"I'm sorry, Harmony," I said.

"Me too, Juniper. Me too. Tess was all I had in this world."

"You really think Leo had something to do with it?" I hoped I wasn't poking a bear with the question.

"Has he told you about Tess?"

"What does he have to tell me about?"

Leo sighed and shook his head. The color returned to his face. He threw a few hundred-dollar bills on the table. Far more than the cost of our dinner. "Let's give Harmony some peace. She's gone through a lot."

"Are you going to tell me about Tess?"

Leo nodded. He looked around at the other people in the restaurant, who were staring at us. A few people along the boardwalk had stopped to watch our spectacle. He spoke through gritted teeth. "In the car."

We walked away. I looked back to see Harmony standing there, continuing to stew. With her bright red hair, she reminded me of an actual volcano erupting. The surrounding murmur grew, as people didn't try to hide their stares or lower their voices.

When we reached KG outside, I had to ask. "What was that all about?"

He shook his head. "I had forgotten that Harmony owned the Indigo Room."

"So, what's the deal between you and Tess?"

He nodded slowly as we climbed back into KG. "I kept catching Tess performing at different local venues. She had such an amazing voice. It became a game. Since I kept running into her all over southern Maryland, we started getting dinner and drinks together after her sets," he said.

"She told me about her desire to perform but that her family didn't think she should pursue a career as a musician. I know what it's like for a family not to support your dreams, so I offered to help her get started. She refused to accept any money from me, saying she'd figure it out her own way. I don't think she wanted to be obligated to anyone." He looked forlorn.

"Were you more than friends?" I started up KG, and we headed back towards the inn. The sky was turning a dusty pink with splashes of purple. It reminded me of Nana Z's watercolor paintings.

"Of course not. But she was fun to be with. And so talented. I'm going to miss her."

I took a gulp of air and finally asked the question that had been bugging me. "On Friday night, I saw someone who looked like you chasing after Tess when she left the Purple Oyster. Was that you?"

Leo sighed and then nodded. "Yeah, I hadn't seen her since she turned down my offer to help, so I wanted to find out what was going on."

"Did you talk with her?"

"I called out to her several times, but she didn't respond. I saw her climb into a car and drive off. I've gathered that most of the town thinks Rory killed Tess and is now hiding somewhere. But I'm pretty sure that Harmony found out about my friendship with Tess and thinks I did it."

I was half tempted to ask if he did, but that wouldn't answer anything. It made me realize how little I knew about Leo. I didn't think he was a murderer, but what did I know? Perhaps he killed Tess to get her family's diary and find the *Book of Kells* covers for the family collection? That seemed far-fetched, but what if finding them would make him a hero in his family's eyes? That didn't seem as far-fetched, especially after hearing him talk about his brother's efforts to do the same thing. I kept my thoughts to myself for now, but I had to figure out a way to investigate them. Was I riding to my sister's inn with a killer?

Chapter Fifteen

Leo dropped me off at the inn with a fairly chaste hug. I was hesitant to give him that after what he had told me. I promised him I would think about what he had said.

It had been a long weekend, and I was exhausted. I wanted to head over to the Carriage House and collapse on my sleeping bag.

Inside, Keisha was at the desk. Clover ran over from camping at her feet. He really looked like he belonged here. Keisha jumped up when she saw me and said, "Juniper! Juniper!"

"You're here pretty late?"

"Well, I….. Oh, wow, your dress is spectacular." I twirled around in it, and she gave an appreciative clap. "Beautiful. You look straight out of the past. Like a movie star."

"Ahh, thank you." I gave a curtsy. "Okay, so what did you need?"

Her face reddened. "I know you told me not to keep searching online—"

"But you did it, anyway?" I asked. She nodded. I sighed and threw my hands up in the air. I came over and joined her behind the front desk, where she had both the inn's computer and her own.

"So look at this." She pulled up a page that looked like some sort of online bidding website. Except it wasn't a company I'd ever seen before. I saw nothing explaining what it was. "They were selling the O'Doyle diary."

"I'm sorry, what?"

"Tess and Rory. Or one of them. Or someone else. I don't know who, but someone was selling the diary on this shadow site. See, that's their avatar there." She pointed to the username, which read "KELLS." It had a picture of a Celtic-looking knot next to it. At first glance, the website looked more like a forum than a traditional auction site, but after skimming through a few threads, I saw what she meant. KELLS had opened a bidding war on the O'Doyle diary, promising that it would lead the owner to the long-lost covers of the *Book of Kells*.

"It looks like there were multiple people bidding," Keisha said. I noted other usernames who'd made fairly large bids. PROFTREASURE was undoubtedly Orson Bradford, but I wasn't sure who the others were. There was PRINCESS84 and BLACKSHEEP. I wondered if BLACKSHEEP might be a reference to Leo. I remembered what he had said about how he was the black sheep of his family. But, I reminded myself, "black sheep" was a pretty generic term, and there was no easy way to trace it to him. Our brains sought connections and patterns, even when there weren't any. It provided little solace.

However, the strangest username was labeled simply "LEA." My heart beat faster upon reading that. Lea was Azalea's nickname. Yet, how could Azalea be on here? That was impossible. I couldn't imagine a universe where Azalea would know how to find a site like this, let alone bid on anything. Could she have somehow learned about the sale and was trying to snoop on Rory? I still didn't know how he was involved in this. Maybe he was masquerading as her?

I lumped myself onto a stool behind Keisha. My brain was going into full-on conspiracy theory mode, trying to make connections every which way, making me somewhat sick.

"Looks like the sale ended on Friday. The seller was supposed to meet the winner that same night," Keisha said.

"At the cemetery?" I asked. I tried remembering everything Rory had told me over the phone when we had chatted on Friday morning. Had he gotten in over his head with this online auction? The bidding war must have been ending soon when he reached out. I wondered if he had got cold feet about whatever his and Tess's plan was. Had he worried the diary was a fake? Was he hoping I could somehow allay his fears? Maybe he was afraid of what would happen if it turned out the diary wasn't what they claimed it was? Was that why he needed me so badly?

"It doesn't say. Just that they'd be in touch with details."

I scrolled through further, trying to see who had won the O'Doyle diary. I assumed it would be PROFTREASURE given all his bombastic announcements, but while he was in the lead, someone else had swooped in at the very end. LEA made a shockingly large bid. A bid that could buy a house not just in Rose Mallow but also in Washington, D.C. This couldn't possibly be Azalea. The name had to be a coincidence. Maybe it was someone's initials? Or someone else's nickname?

"How did the winner pay the seller? I can't imagine a site like this takes credit cards," I asked Keisha.

"I'm not really sure. Maybe through some sort of cryptocurrency? Or maybe the black market has its own payment processor?" She shrugged as if this was a normal conversation. "We should call Detective Gupta. She needs to see this."

"Let's tell Azalea first." I hated that what I truly wanted to see was how she would respond to seeing LEA. That thought left my stomach twisting.

"Sure, she has a right to know."

"What do I have a right to know?" Azalea appeared. I waved her over. "What am I looking at?"

"Someone placed the O'Doyle diary up for a bidding war," I explained.

"What? When?" She sounded surprised. It sounded sincere to me, but to be fair, I was pretty biased. There was no way that Azalea could be involved. There had to be a more reasonable explanation. I just didn't know it yet.

"It started a few weeks ago and then ended on Friday," said Keisha.

Azalea shook her head. "Oh no. Does that mean?"

"Maybe," I replied, knowing full well she was asking the same question we had been wondering. Was the winner Tess's killer?

"What have the police said about this?"

"I don't know if they know yet," I replied.

"What? Then how did you find out? What website is this?"

"Well, um, it's definitely not eBay. I think it's a black market site," I said.

Azalea opened her mouth to ask another question when the truth dawned on her. She turned to Keisha. "Did you find this?" When Keisha nodded, Azalea turned to me. "And you knew about this?"

"Not exactly. I knew she was looking around online, but I didn't know about finding any sort of dark websites."

"I can't believe you, Juniper. I trusted you to look into things, but I never thought you would rake in a teenager. You could have gotten Keisha into a lot of trouble. She might still get in trouble. Who knows what kind of tracking this has or who these people are? We know someone was killed already." As Azalea went on, her voice got louder, and I watched as Keisha's demeanor went from wanting to fight back to wanting to cry. I felt the same way. What had I done?

"We're about to call Detective Gupta," I said sheepishly.

"Good. But after that, I want you to stay out of it until things are settled. I should never have encouraged you to look into Rory's disappearance. That is on me, but you should have told me about Keisha." She shook her head. She spoke with such quiet determination. I felt utterly destroyed.

"Hey, I'm not a kid," Keisha said.

"That may be, but you're also not yet an adult. And you're my employee using my internet. Do you want me to tell your parents what you've done? Or your sister?" Azalea asked. Keisha quit her argument quickly and shook her head briskly. "For now, let's call Detective Gupta."

"Before we do, there's something you should see." I pointed to the username LEA. Azalea looked closely at the screen.

"Well, that's a weird coincidence."

"I'm not sure if Detective Gupta will see it that way."

"It's three letters. It could be almost anything. If I had been on here, why would I use something so obvious? I think I'd select something else to obscure my identity," she replied. I both agreed with her and wondered how she thought of something so crafty, so quickly.

"Pretty sure PROFTREASURE is that TV guy," Keisha said.

"Yeah, well, that's him, not me." Azalea rolled her eyes.

I pulled out my phone and called the detective. Once again, she answered immediately. I explained what we had found, and she asked us to take screenshots of the site. She said she'd get them over to her team. Keisha pulled the screenshots right away. I wanted to stop her from taking any that included LEA, but I knew it wasn't something we could get away with hiding.

After finishing up, Azalea sent Keisha home. I piddled around, wondering what I should do. Finally, I announced, "I'm going to go pack up. I'll find a hotel for the night and head out after talking to the detective tomorrow."

Azalea sighed. "Look, I'm just not happy with you involving Keisha in your antics."

"Antics? You asked me to investigate." I didn't like that she had given over all the blame to me. I should have pushed back harder on Keisha snooping online, but I didn't think she had done anything particularly unsafe. It wasn't like Azalea had been overseeing things herself.

"Yes, I asked *you*. Not anyone else," she clarified.

I wanted to make a retort about her moping around, but I bit my tongue. She didn't need me lashing out at her. "I'm going back to the Carriage House. I'll be gone by the morning." I'd hoped Azalea would stop me and take back her threat, but she didn't. Instead, I walked back through the house to the garden with a heavy heart. An exhausted one, too.

All I wanted to do was change out of my dress and into some comfy pajamas. It was getting late, and I needed sleep. The idea of packing up and finding a hotel wasn't appealing. I debated if I could go first thing in the morning. Clearly, I needed to give Azalea some space. Going tonight would be the best option.

It took until I was almost at the Carriage House to notice the spray paint. Someone had written "GO AWAY!" across the door. I was more annoyed than scared.

"Of course. Great," I said to the door. "Does anyone think this can wait until morning?" I took a few photos with my phone. I didn't think they turned out great in the darkness, but it was the best I could do at the moment. Then, I checked out the inside of the Carriage House. The door was still locked, which seemed to be a positive sign, at least. None of the windows were broken or ajar either. Inside, I flipped on every light switch and called out through the rooms. Everything inside seemed in order, or well, as much order as all the boxes allowed. Nothing seemed to have moved or been touched.

"Any chance it's just teenagers?" I wondered aloud. I knew better, though. After the incident with KG and everything else this weekend, I knew it was another message. If I had harbored any hope that the last one had been misdirected, this time affirmed the truth. Someone was trying to stop me.

Could Rory have done this? Would he have done it? Why would he risk coming out here to vandalize my things while he was still missing? If it wasn't him, though, then who?

I gazed back at the main house. I imagined Azalea and Violet asleep inside. I had caused my sister enough pain. I didn't need to add to it. We would deal with this in the morning. I knew I couldn't leave them. Not yet, anyway. Instead, I locked the door and pushed a chair against it. I made sure everything else was locked as well. Then, I crawled up into the sleeping bag and fell asleep hard.

Chapter Sixteen

"Juniper! Juniper!"

"Bark! Woof!"

I woke up with a start. It was surprisingly sunny inside the overloaded Carriage House. Great, I had slept in a lot later than I had planned. Plus, I was still in Nana Z's vintage Dior dress. In all the chaos last night, I had forgotten to change. It was now a wrinkly mess stuck in every different direction. At least I'd kicked off the heels.

"Juniper!"

I pulled the chair away from the door and opened it slowly, not happy about all that bright morning sunshine streaming in. On the other side was Detective Gupta, a couple other deputies I didn't recognize, and a very unhappy-looking Azalea. I guessed she had learned about the vandalism. I noted that Deputy Torres wasn't here. Clover raced in and jumped all over me, adding dirt to the already messed up dress.

"Good morning," I said with a yawn. I reached down to pet Clover.

"Did you know about this?" Azalea asked, pointing to the spray paint. I peeked outside, unsure if I should be upfront or not yet. In the end, I chose honesty.

"I'm sorr...." Before I could get the words out, Azalea rushed in and enveloped me in a powerful hug.

"I'm just glad you're okay," she whispered. I nodded into her shoulder. She didn't let go. Clover jumped up on our legs. "I never should have told you to leave. There's obviously someone out there angry about you."

"I'm so sorry, Azalea." I felt like I was constantly apologizing. It would have been nice if I could figure out how not to need to do that anymore, especially to my sister.

"Excuse me, ladies?" Detective Gupta interrupted us. We pulled apart. Detective Gupta eyed my eccentric ensemble with uncertainty. I suspected that my hair and face were an overwhelming mess. "Why don't we give Juniper here a few minutes to freshen up for the day? I'll meet you in the library in ten."

I changed as quickly as I could, digging out a jersey sundress that didn't seem in too bad of shape. I washed my face and brushed back my hair. Fortunately, my bob was getting to be long enough that I could tie it back, which would have to be good enough for this morning.

Most of the deputies were outside the Carriage House door as I left. Some came in and looked around the place. I hoped they wouldn't go through my things, but at least there was nothing to hide in my duffel bag.

"Where's the TV crew?" I asked Azalea as she bandied about the kitchen.

"Already left to go to the archaeological site. Just us. Violet's still asleep."

Detective Gupta waited in the same chair in the library as she had sat in on Saturday. Azalea again came in with a tray of chocolate babka slices and a pot of tea. I suspected the babka was another one of Nana Z's recipes, as we'd grown up with it for most holidays. Instead of lingering around the periphery, she sat down on the sofa and patted the cushion next to her for me to join her.

"Well, this continues to be an interesting weekend," Detective Gupta said. She picked up a slice of babka and took a bite into it. She stopped and stared at the gooey slice in amazement. Azalea looked pleased as she leaped up to pour some tea for all three of us.

"That's one way to put it," I replied as I took a slice of babka as well. I wasn't going to miss out on its rich brioche or creamy chocolate filling. "Did you know that Leo Calverton tried giving money to Tess O'Doyle?"

The detective dropped her babka back onto a plate.

Azalea turned her gaze to me and poured right past the cup, getting tea all over her serving tray. I swallowed a laugh.

"I've been wondering if this could all be related to the death of her grandfather too."

"Whose grandfather?" Detective Gupta said in between swallowing bites.

"Tess's. Her grandfather was Bobby O'Doyle. He drowned in the Chesapeake Bay in 1959 while also looking for the *Book of Kells* covers. Apparently, the rumor of these covers has existed for centuries. However, no one has ever found them."

"Wait, go back to Calverton and O'Doyle."

"Right. They were friends, although I think Harmony believes they were something more. He says they weren't dating, but he tried supporting her music career with money, and she turned down his offer. I don't know if Harmony believes him. She seems to think he's a prime candidate." I felt slightly bad going on about Leo this much. I really enjoyed my date with him. However, before things could possibly go further, I had to know that he was innocent.

The detective was quiet for a few moments. "Did Calverton say anything about the diary Tess was auctioning off? Did she tell him why she was selling it?"

"No. I didn't know about the auction yet when I learned about his friendship with her, though. It sounds like she cut off things and without a lot of details," I replied before taking a bite of babka. It was as good as any Nana Z had made. Azalea watched me try it. I nodded at her with a sprawling smile, and she seemed to breathe a sigh of relief.

"That is all very interesting. I'll look into it. However, I'm here primarily to talk with Azalea," the detective said.

"Me? What else can I tell you?"

"Mainly, I wanted you to know we traced the LEA username back to an IP address out of this house," Detective Gupta said.

I was gobsmacked. Was the detective implying my sister was involved with Tess's death? All because I had allowed Keisha to snoop online? "There has to be a good reason."

"I...I don't know why." Azalea looked stunned.

"Did you win the O'Doyle diary?" the detective asked her.

"I didn't know about the diary until Saturday."

"You have a young daughter, is that correct?"

"Yes. She's Rory's daughter, too." There was a desperation in Azalea's voice that frightened me.

"Can you find someone to care for her?"

"Why?"

"Because I need you to come to the station with me."

"Are you arresting her?" I practically screamed.

"That depends," she said.

"On what?"

"Her answers to some questions. Look, you have the most motivation, Azalea," Detective Gupta said. As she spoke, she punctuated each statement with hand gestures. "You were going through a divorce. You claimed that Rory had harassed you with crushed flowers and creepy messages. Then, he starts dating a new woman. A younger woman. Perhaps he was taunting you with that, too. And then you learned they were selling this diary for an outrageous amount of money. Not only was he hurting you, but he was going to become rich."

I grabbed Azalea's hand as she talked. Her face went pale. I worried she might pass out. I half worried that I would, too.

Detective Gupta continued, saying, "You bought the O'Doyle diary, but you never intended to pay that ridiculous sum. Instead, you met the both of them in the cemetery and took your revenge there and then. You killed Tess, and maybe you've killed Rory, too. I'm guessing your sister showing up interrupted your hiding of Tess's body as well?"

"That can't be. That can't be right," I responded for her. Then, I noticed the deputies were surrounding us. This wasn't good. I wanted to steal Azalea away as they circled us. "What about the vandalism? Azalea didn't do that."

"Didn't she? She never counted on you being here, Juniper. She was trying to scare you to leave."

"She wouldn't do any of that." I tried to think quickly, but I didn't know what to say or do. Azalea listened, appearing to go comatose. "Wait, what about the flowers?"

"What flowers?" Detective Gupta asked.

"There were more crushed flowers *after* Rory disappeared."

"That was Azalea. Covering her tracks." The detective had a defiant glint, as if she was daring me to come up with a way to upset her theory. I was struggling, practically flailing, but Azalea appeared to have given up entirely.

Azalea turned to me and said in a far-away voice. "Take Violet to Keisha's parents. They'll make sure she's okay until we get this sorted out. I'm sure they'll hold on to Clover too if you need."

"What? No."

"Juniper, please. Don't fight me on this. Not right now. We'll get it sorted out."

"Then I'm going to stay too to help."

"Don't you have to get back to D.C. to work?"

"The Library of Congress can wait. I'll be here as long as you need."

Naturally, it was at the same time that my phone dinged with yet another text, with another demand from Greyson. I wondered if I could block him temporarily until this all got figured out.

"Okay, but only if you're sure."

"Azalea. I'm not leaving you when you're being arrested."

"They haven't arrested me yet. I'm just going to answer some questions at the station. Right, Detective?" Azalea asked.

The detective shrugged noncommittally.

"What about the Chronos Channel crew?" I asked.

"Ask Keisha if Desiree can help, too. Between the two of them, I think we'll be alright."

"Okay. What about you? Do you have a lawyer?" I asked.

Azalea blinked at the question. Then she nodded. "Yeah, my divorce lawyer. Maxwell Turner. His number is in the drawer in the kitchen. You know the one." I knew exactly what she meant. Nana Z kept a book with an embroidered fabric cover with phone numbers in the same kitchen drawer for decades.

Azalea went with the detective and deputies. As they walked out, Detective Gupta turned to me and said, "If you want to help your sister, stay out of trouble."

"If I want to help her, I need to find out who really killed Tess," I replied, hoping I sounded more confident than I felt.

"If I hear you're interfering with anything—anything at all—I'm coming back with another deputy to arrest you." I knew she would keep her word.

They didn't handcuff Azalea or place her formally under arrest, but she was guided to the back of a police car. I couldn't decide if she looked serene or stunned as she sat back there.

Some neighbors watched from their porches. Cordelia was on her porch. She stood with crossed her arms and wore a fairly smug smile. I slammed the door on my way back into the inn. At least Whitney wasn't there to witness my sister being carted away.

Chapter Seventeen

Once everyone was gone, I called Keisha and updated her about everything. I warned her not to tell Violet that anything was wrong. As we talked, I poked my head into the little girl's makeshift bedroom to check that she was still asleep.

"No worries. I've babysat for her at least a million times," Keisha said. "I'll be over in a few minutes."

"And Desiree? Is she working at the shop today?"

"I think she'll understand it's an emergency. What are you going to do?" she asked.

"I don't know yet. I'm still figuring that out."

Honestly, I didn't have a clue what my next step was except to call Maxwell Turner. I headed back to the kitchen and pulled out Nana Z's phone book. Azalea had been updating it. I found his number under T for Turner, Turner, & Turner.

"Maxwell," he said when he answered. He sounded like I'd woken him up.

"Hi, this is Azalea Blume's sister Juniper."

"Sure, sure." He then yawned loudly.

"She's been arrested. Or is about to be."

Silence.

"Hello? Mr. Turner?"

"Did you say Azalea has been arrested?" He sounded far more awake now.

"Well, about to be."

"What are they arresting her for?"

I hated to say it, but what choice did I have? "They think she killed Tess

O'Doyle. And maybe Rory, too."

"They found his body?" Now, his words were sharp and precise.

"No, I don't think so. But they think she killed him and somehow disposed of his body. And that I interrupted her doing the same to Tess."

"Is she at the station?"

"They left a few minutes ago."

"Okay, I'm on my way." He hung up. I texted Azalea that he was coming and that Keisha and Desiree would take care of Violet. She didn't respond, so I couldn't tell if she got my message or not.

Once the sisters arrived, I headed back to the Calverton Golf Club to find Orson. He might not be happy to see me, but I wanted to know what he knew about the online auction for the diary.

The media vans weren't there. I didn't have any trouble with the guards getting onto the site. I suspected that was partially Leo's doing.

"What are you doing here?" Ruth stopped me as I walked onto the site. Just beyond her, a series of pink flags announced the different locations for shovel test pits. The archaeologists were already working on a few. The TV crew lounged in the back, not really paying any attention. I didn't see Orson anywhere.

"Orson never got the O'Doyle diary," I said.

"What are you talking about?"

"He lost the auction."

Her aggression shifted into a look of surprise, but it didn't strike me as sincere. "What auction?"

"Oh, come off it. PROFTREASURE? Not very original."

"How do you know about that?" Her voice betrayed her nervousness.

"You were the one bidding." I was sure of it. She did everything else for him. I suspected she orchestrated this entire campaign. I couldn't imagine Orson having the understanding for doing any of this.

"How did you know?" Her shoulders slumped forward, and her head hung down.

"He relies on you. Even if he had taken part in the auction, you still would have been the one to place the bids. So if you didn't win, how did you get the diary pages?"

Ruth sighed. To my surprise, she pulled out a pack of cigarettes and lit one. As much as I was disgusted by the smell, I didn't stop her. "You don't remember me, do you?"

"Do we know each other?" I hadn't expected that.

"Yeah, I've discovered most people around here don't seem to remember little Ruthie Dawson. I changed it to Collins in college. That was my mother's maiden name." She paused for a moment and looked at me, but I still didn't recognize her, although the last name struck a bell. "I was a couple of grades behind you. And a good bit heavier back then. With thick Coke-bottle glasses and some hand-me-down clothes. You all certainly wouldn't let me forget any of that."

The memories flooded back to me. I hadn't seen it before, but she was the kid sister of Tommy Dawson—the same boy I had kissed for the first time in Tidewater Cemetery. He had been part of our summer group of teens—the same group that included Rory, Whitney, Azalea, and myself. There had been several others who flitted in and out over the summer. We had often tried to get rid of Ruthie. I hadn't realized at the time what a bully we had been to Ruthie.

"Oh my. I'm so, so sorry, Ruthie…I mean, Ruth."

Ruth puffed away on her cigarette. "Water under the bridge." She looked towards the excavation in progress. "Who do you think told Orson about Rose Mallow in the first place?" That made sense. She must have known about the town's long-fabled connection to the *Book of Kells*.

"So you discovered the bidding war?"

"I kept an eye out for things about the *Book of Kells* and Rose Mallow."

"But you didn't win."

"We didn't. However, there was enough information to figure out where the exchange was going to go down. I tried going out to the cemetery early, figuring I'd convince them to sell to us," she said.

"You must have gotten there before I did."

"We must have been ships passing in the night, then. When I got there, I didn't see anyone. But I saw the O'Doyle diary. It was sitting on one of the gravestones. I snapped a few pictures of the pages inside. I was going to take it when I heard something and ran off. That must have been you coming into the cemetery," she said.

"You didn't see Rory or Tess?"

"No. But, it doesn't mean that they weren't there. It was dark, and it was also very quiet. I hated it. I've always hated cemeteries and cemeteries at night." She visibly shuddered and groaned. "I hightailed it out of there as soon as I could manage."

"Do you still have the photos? How many pages did you get?"

She pulled out her phone and flipped through. There were close to twenty photos there of different pages. They weren't the best pictures in the world, having been taken hurriedly at night, but they were in better shape than I could have dared hope. The photo of the map was in the best condition, which reminded me of the blown-up image at the press conference.

"Where is the big version of the map you had printed?" I asked.

"Oh, I'm not sure. Probably in the Foundation somewhere. Leo is storing things for us."

"That makes sense." I whipped out my phone and texted him. He responded almost immediately, saying he'd meet us at the Foundation in three minutes. He was finishing up an early morning run. I headed that way, but Ruth held back. "Aren't you coming?"

"I don't think so. We have a lot to do here." She took another drag on her cigarette.

"I need what's on your phone," I said.

"I'll text them to you." Ruth threw the butt at the ground and rubbed it out with her shoe. I wasn't sure why she wore designer heels to a dig site. However, she had kept them immaculate.

"I could use you," I said.

Ruth huffed. "Okay, fine. But if Orson calls me, I'm out."

"Of course." We headed over to the Golf Club's restaurant when Leo came running up. He wasn't wearing a shirt. Beads of sweat draped across his remarkably sculpted and tanned torso. A few locks of his raven dark hair were slightly out of place. I wondered if anyone else noticed me staring before I caught myself. It took me a second to pop back up my dropped jaw. I did a quick scan of my hurriedly assembled outfit from this morning and wished I could rush back home and maybe hide in bed.

"So what do you need?" he asked.

"Those big prints of the O'Doyle diary and its map. And I want to see what other maps you have of the area—as old as you can go," I replied.

"I have more diary pics," Ruth said. Leo's eyebrows raised. I don't think he had expected that. "It's a long story."

"Okay, then let me get you both in the archives room, and I'll change up."

Within ten minutes, we were settled in the reading room of the Foundation's library. Unlike the 19th century gilded age look of the Library of Congress's main reading room, the Foundation's was sleek and modern. Windows surrounded us, although they had obviously been tinted and coated with a UV filter to reduce the sun's impact on the delicate documents. The room was a deep slate gray with dark wooden tables and Eames chairs.

Leo appeared, quickly dressed and looking as if he had not just been running in the thick Chesapeake heat. He soon pulled out every 17th-century map the Foundation had of Maryland. Some listed Rose Mallow, but most didn't. Many were quite large, so we put each one at a different table to spread out safely. While I scanned through the maps, Leo worked with Ruth on printing large copies of every photo she had snagged of the O'Doyle diary.

The Foundation owned copies of John Smith's 1612 map of the Chesapeake Bay and the 1635 map by Jerome Hawley and John Lewger. However, it wasn't until I got to John Ogilby's 1671 map of the Chesapeake area that a realization struck. I had seen the Ogilby map several times when I visited the Maryland State Archives. A large copy graced the walls of their reading room. It tended to surprise everyone because Maryland and the Chesapeake weren't oriented North and South like the maps we have today. Instead, the New World was presented from a mariner's point of view, traveling into the Bay from its mouth and heading across in what appeared to be sideways. In all three antique maps, Maryland would have looked sideways to modern eyes.

I ran over to the printout of the O'Doyle diary's map. What if it had been oriented incorrectly? And what if the shoreline had moved over the past 350 years? That was why Bobby O'Doyle had thought the covers were in the Chesapeake Bay. I felt awful that he had drowned trying to reach them underwater. However, I suspected that while he was on the right track, he wasn't quite right either. They weren't at the Golf Course, though. If I was adjusting the map to modern terrain correctly, then they were somewhere part of its neighbor: the ruins of the Baytastic Amusement Park and Zoo.

Leo and Ruth chattered as they returned to the reading room. I debated telling them. As much as I didn't want to believe that either was the killer, I didn't know that for certain yet. However, one thing bothered me. Wouldn't the killer have taken the O'Doyle diary with them?

A second realization dawned on me. I knew who had killed Tess, and if I was right, then it was possible that Rory was still alive.

Chapter Eighteen

"I need to go," I practically shouted at them.

"Where are you going?" Leo asked.

"Back to the inn. Unless you have some dark-haired wigs or nicer clothes I could borrow."

"Sure, my sister has almost a storage unit full of them. Why?" he asked. I almost stopped to ask why on earth his sister would have a storage unit full of wigs, but there wasn't time to ponder what the children of billionaires used their money on.

"I need to look like Azalea," I replied.

"That's weird," Ruth said.

"Yes, but we need to hurry. Rory's life depends on it."

"Wait, wait, wait. Slow down. Explain what you're talking about," Leo said.

"Lead me to the storage unit. I'll explain my plan along the way."

As we headed to the storage unit, I told Leo and Ruth my plan, which they didn't like. They wanted to call the police immediately. Leo offered to send a security staff detail with me.

I pushed back. "Give me fifteen minutes. I need to find Rory and draw out the killer. Once I do that, you can bring the guns a-blazing."

"You're going to get yourself killed," Leo argued.

"Wait." Ruth snapped her fingers. "What if she wears a wire or a walkie-talkie or something? It can be a sting operation."

I nodded. "Yes, I can do that."

"Fine," replied Leo. He crossed his arms, obviously not fully on board with our plan. However, he had not been kidding about the storage unit. His sister had three rooms set aside just for clothing and accessories. "She likes the climate control we have here."

"Wow, this is even more wigs than I had expected," I said.

"Remember the movie *Clueless*? Annie is a lot like Alicia Silverstone's character. She loves her clothes. She likes to sport a different look every day of the year."

This was more than love, but I didn't have time to think about that now. I raced through the first room and found a wig with shoulder-length dark brown hair. Azalea wore a preppier style compared to me, so I did my best to snag a few articles like that. Once transformed, I checked myself out in a wall mirror. If someone didn't know better, they would have thought I was Azalea.

We headed over to where the Park and Zoo met the cemetery. "Fifteen minutes. That's it."

"Wouldn't the police have already checked those places?" Ruth asked.

"I'm sure they have, but if I'm right, Rory was hidden at the time," I explained. "Since they crossed it off their list, there's no reason to hide him anymore." Instead, I assumed that the kidnapper simply wanted Rory trapped. If they'd wanted him dead, I figured we would have found him by now.

"I don't like this plan," Leo replied.

"If we all go in together, Rory is dead. Trust me."

Leo considered what I said. Then he pulled me over and kissed me hard. I was surprised, but quickly melted into his kiss. My resolve began slipping away, but I shook my head and pulled away. There would be time for kisses later. I hoped anyway.

"If you think this will work," Leo said, "then I think so too." I smiled at his vote of confidence.

"Well, I think it's a foolhardy and dumb idea," said Ruth. She dug out another cigarette and wagged it at me. "But I've seen enough people with foolhardy and dumb ideas succeed where the rest of us fail. Orson proves that on a nearly daily basis."

"Thank you, I think."

I slipped into the Baytastic Amusement Park and Zoo. The place had been a favorite summer hangout when I was young. Sure, it had been out of date even then with its faded and peeling paint, but what kid or teen would have cared? They had made the best funnel cakes and had the fastest roller coasters. I remembered winning an oversized duck from one of the carnival games, which I had named Alfred for some odd reason.

I came across the Zoo portion of Baytastic. Built back in 1887, the cages here looked almost like medieval torture devices. There were round metal cages, nearly covered with ivy and kudzu, attached to dark stone buildings, now half collapsed.

As a teenager, Azalea and I went on big group dates with all the local kids to this place. I remembered one night I had lost Azalea for over an hour. Eventually, I found her snuggling with Rory over a giant cotton candy. They were inseparable after that.

However, Azalea wasn't the only kid we lost for a few hours that night. As much as I found their relationship nauseating, someone else had found it devastating. We found our other missing friend back here among the zoo portion.

I tested out the tiny lavalier microphone that Leo had hooked me up with. It connected to a receiver and worked through my phone. Supposedly, they could hear me, but I couldn't hear them. We had tried rigging up a pair of earbuds, but our quick attempt didn't succeed. I prayed that the one-way transmission did.

"Can you hear me? I'm in the zoo part. I think this is where Rory will be."

I wondered if it was safe to call out for Rory. I decided against it. Besides, I was fairly confident I knew where he was. I walked through the maze of cages but didn't see any signs of life.

"C'mon, Rory. Please be here, please be here."

The sun beat down on me. I had hoped with the water nearby, there'd be some relief from the heat, but it made things worse. I worried I was sweating so much the wig would fall off my head.

"Where is it?" I continued working through the mess. Half of the signs had been bleached out to where I couldn't read what animal had been where.

It didn't help anything that it'd been over fifteen years or so since I had last visited this place. However, the muscle memory from tearing through here for all those summers hadn't completely disappeared.

Towards the end of the cages, I found the one I had been searching for: the old tiger's enclosure. Sure enough, I found Rory locked inside. He lay across the concrete slab, completely exposed to the heat and weather. His chest moved slowly as he breathed heavily. He was alive, but not in great shape. When he spotted me, he lifted his head a little.

I whispered into my mic, "I found Rory. He's in the tiger cage at the very back of the zoo. He's alive, but he needs medical attention."

"Azalea? Oh, Azalea. I... I love you. I'm so sorry. I want to go home." His voice was dry. I didn't bother correcting him, seeing how hurt and frail he appeared. Besides, I was disguised as Azalea, after all.

Instead, I replied, "We'll find you a way out."

"It's my fault. All this divorce stuff. I'm so sorry for not being there for you how you needed me to be."

"It's okay, Rory."

"If I make it out of here alive, I want to make things right with you. Please."

"You're going to make it out of here just fine. We'll figure it out."

However, as soon as I finished speaking, Baytastic's ancient P.A. system sparked into life. "Azalea Blume!"

I circled around in space, trying to see how I was spotted. The sun was hot and heavy this morning, and I struggled to find where the voice originated. However, even through the crackling of the system, I knew exactly who it belonged to.

"I knew it. I knew the divorce thing was a scam." Whitney Sullivan's voice laughed bitterly. It reverberated throughout the park.

Whitney had witnessed Azalea and Rory's first kiss that night in the park and had run off afterwards in tears. Park security was called in to help locate her. We eventually found Whitney curled up and sobbing behind the tiger's cage. A zookeeper – barely older than we were—discovered her back there, in a staff-only section. We were scolded and reminded of how Whitney could have been seriously hurt. She had been banned from Baytastic for the rest of that summer. During that time, Azalea and Rory's relationship had flourished.

"It's Whitney Sullivan. Whitney Sullivan kidnapped Rory," I told the microphone.

"You thought you could take him from me. Take everything from me."

A shot was fired, narrowly missing me. I darted for cover behind a half-fallen wooden stand. I suspected it had once sold souvenirs. Looking up, I caught the glint of metal from atop the tallest roller coaster, the Baytastic Bombardier. The coaster was a wooden contraption that towered over most of the park. I was amazed it hadn't yet collapsed like so much of the rest of the place. Whitney was up there, holding a rifle in one hand and a microphone in another.

"Come down, Whitney. You can still make this right," I yelled out.

"You're going to take him from me. Again. Like that harpy at the coffee shop."

She must have seen Tess and Rory together recently. I remembered how harshly she'd spoken to Tess at the Purple Oyster. I suspected that's what had finally set her off. I figured she had hoped he would turn to her when he and Azalea broke up, and it must have devastated her when she saw him turn to Tess instead.

Another shot was fired. This one went wide. I snuck a glance upwards. Whitney was preparing to fire again. For the first time in my entire life, I wished I had a gun. Not that I would have known what to do with it. My only experience was shooting balloons with the fake rifles in the Park's arcade and those toys would not help me now.

"If he won't be with me, then he won't be with anyone."

"What about your boyfriend, Georgie?" I called out, hoping I had remembered the name correctly. "I'm sure he loves you and wants you home."

"I lied. There's no boyfriend. Stupid pig sent me flowers to dump me after I failed the bar exam. I have nothing." Whitney sounded desperate. Ah, the "GEO" on the scrap of paper with the flowers. Those must have come from him.

"You have your grandmother," I argued.

"That old bat? She hates me, and I hate her. I can't wait to dump her on someone else. I came back to be near Rory after Azalea set him loose. If he won't be with me now, I don't have anything." After losing her boyfriend and failing the bar, Whitney must have felt lost. I assumed that hearing Rory might be available must have given her a mooring to latch onto.

I almost felt bad for her, but seeing as she was the one camped out shooting at us with a rifle and keeping Rory in a cage, I couldn't really muster up any sympathy. I needed to get Rory out of here. Or at least distract Whitney until the authorities arrived. I checked my watch. My fifteen minutes were nearly up, but I was still on my own for a few more.

"Azalea." Rory's voice was weak and hoarse. "Get out of here! Save yourself!"

"Not without you," I replied, although I wasn't sure he could hear me.

Whitney had created a station for herself atop the roller coaster. It undoubtedly gave her a good view of the entire park and zoo, including the cage where she held Rory captive. Plus, she had strung the microphone up there in some way. She must have been planning to make a stand there for some time.

That meant there was still electricity running in this section. How else would the P.A. work or the car have gotten up there? Getting over to the roller coaster meant racing through a partially exposed aisle between various collapsed and rotting carnival stands. I didn't want to leave Rory, but I couldn't help him from where I hid.

First, I took off the wig. My apologies to Leo's sister, but I figured she had more wigs at her disposal if she needed another. I hung it on the back of the stand, trying to make it seem like I, or well, my sister, was hiding there and partially exposed.

Next, I pulled out my new phone and gave it a small apology. "I've had you less than two days, but I suspect that's all I'm going to get." I hoped Leo and Ruth had received enough information from me that they wouldn't need me to update them anymore. Assuming it had worked at all. Well, at least there wouldn't be any more texts from Greyson to worry about.

I punched up the volume on my phone as loud as it could go and searched for a song to stream with a long, quiet intro that grew gradually into a billowing crescendo. I settled on "Shine On You Crazy Diamond" by Pink Floyd. Seemed appropriate for the situation. I tossed the phone out in front of the stand.

Then, I backed up and while hovered in a ducked position, ran from the scene. As the music kicked in, I heard Whitney call out, "Found you!" She positioned the rifle and shot at my faux location.

Meanwhile, I continued to race across the exposed aisle towards the wooden roller coaster. I wasn't much of a runner, but I suspected I could have won a few international titles with my speed that day. The wooden roller coaster loomed above me like a small mountain. A wire fence stood between me and the coaster. I looked for the thick electrical cords and ran down the fence line, following them. Tall weeds both shielded me and stifled my movement. Eventually, though, I found a fault in the fence and headed inside.

I hated riding roller coasters. I never found them exhilarating, but instead, they made me feel sick to my stomach the few times I had been coerced into trying them. I had always worried they would collapse under me, and looking at this ancient wooden device, I had little confidence it wouldn't.

"Not so fast!" Whitney called out.

A shot ticked off near me. I had been discovered. I was exposed down here, and I wondered if everything was going to end with the next shot. I kept running, moving underneath the mountain of planks that looked to me like they might splinter at any moment. At least I was no longer exposed, as she would have to find me through the crisscross of these overgrown popsicle sticks.

I climbed up onto the roller coaster's starting platform. There was a sign proclaiming how the Baytastic Bombardier was 2,500 feet long with hills reaching as high up as 70 feet. That must be where Whitney's car now sat. Another car waited to be loaded up and start the ride. At the edge of the platform was a control panel with a series of brightly colored buttons. I wondered if they still worked. I assumed the big red one was an emergency stop button, but the nearly as big green one looked tempting. I pressed it and jumped into the waiting car.

The ride started slowly, but it didn't take long to build up speed. I rode through a forest of rickety wooden stems as my car climbed up the track, going faster and faster. The old conveyor belt on the track ahead beneath the car pulled me along. The belt disappeared, and suddenly, my car and I were coasting, flying along as we went down and up along the coaster. My stomach flew along as well, and I wasn't sure I wouldn't throw up. The coaster was a long one, snaking along, and I kept looking up and ahead to see where Whitney was. I didn't know if starting things up had sent her moving or if she was still camped out in the same place.

If I hadn't been so terrified, I might have appreciated the views of the Chesapeake Bay the coaster afforded me. The day was hot, but the sky and water were brilliant shades of blue. If I was going to die, at least it would be with a final spectacular sight.

Then another shot pinged off my car. I looked ahead and saw Whitney's car stuck at the top of the largest hill. It wasn't moving, and I was still picking up speed. We were going to crash at the 70-foot top of the roller coaster, assuming she didn't shoot me first. Ruth had been right. This had been a dumb and foolhardy idea.

Right before we crashed, the ride slowed down. It didn't stop immediately, but the car lost speed, going slower and slower. Whitney watched me approach with surprise and readied her rifle. My car hadn't completely stopped and instead came up, knocking into hers, setting her car loose. Her car had been at the peak of the coaster's tallest hill, and it took little for it to go flying down the other side. She screamed as her car careened through the rest of the ride.

I was right behind her.

My car had slowed to a near stop, but it hadn't stopped all the way, so after her car flew down the track, mine followed. Gravity pulled us along, and as we picked up speed descending the track, we both sailed. The track smoothed out, and we coasted with her still maybe twenty feet ahead of me. She was so focused on her out-of-control car that she had dropped the rifle, although I knew it was still there next to her. Once things slowed down again, I was going to be a goner, but at least she was no longer holed up atop the Bombardier.

As we flew, I saw the platform coming up. Then I knew why my car had slowed down. There was Detective Gupta, Deputy Torres, and a slew of other cops waiting for us. I wanted to jump up and down in celebration. Our cars settled down in front of the platform, with hers reaching there first and mine a few feet behind.

"Come out, Whitney," Detective Gupta said.

"Never!" She stood up in the car, cradling the rifle in her arms, although not in a way that she could actually shoot anyone.

"We have Rory. It's over," she said. I exhaled deeply, grateful that he was finally safe.

"It's not over! Come any closer, and I shoot again!"

"You don't have to do that," Detective Gupta called out.

With Whitney focused on the police, I crept silently out of my car, staying as low as I could. Deputy Torres noticed me, but I put my finger up to my lips. He nodded. I ran along the track, hoping Whitney wouldn't look behind her.

"I'm not going back," Whitney said. "Not without Rory. We're meant to be together!" Her voice shook with rage. She fumbled with the rifle. If I didn't move faster, someone was going to get hurt or worse.

"Come on, Whitney. Put down the rifle. No one's worth this," Detective Gupta said, sounding sympathetic.

Instead of responding, Whitney raised the rifle. At the same time, I reached her car and shoved it hard. The car skidded along the tracks, and the rifle flew from her hands. I caught the back of the car and flew along with it. Whitney fell onto the car's floor as I climbed inside. We both scrambled for the rifle, but I reached it first. The car didn't travel far before settling and slowing to a stop.

"It's over, Whitney," I said, hoping I was holding the rifle properly. I must have been intimidating because Whitney raised her arms in surrender. As she did, the police swarmed the car, taking control. They handcuffed her and carted her out of the park. Meanwhile, I learned that an ambulance had already whisked Rory away for treatment.

I was dizzy and nauseous, but otherwise, unharmed. Deputy Torres helped me back onto the roller coaster's platform, asking, "Are you okay? What were you doing up there?"

"I wanted to help Azalea," I replied.

He nodded in understanding. "Thank you," he said.

Detective Gupta led me back to the primary artery of the park where Leo, Ruth, and Azalea waited for me. Seeing my sister, I ran over and embraced her in an enormous hug, lifting her off the ground.

"Oh, thank goodness you're okay," I said to her.

"I was going to say the same about you. What a horrifically stupid thing to do." She pulled me in tighter as she fussed at me. Then she turned to Leo and Ruth to say, "And I can't believe you two let her do that."

"We called the police," Leo said with a sheepish expression.

Ruth was more defiant. "I've seen stupider things work."

"Could you guys hear me?" I asked, wondering if our makeshift system had worked.

"Uh, for part of the time. We knew you located Rory and that he needed help. Then, the system died. But we had already called the authorities," said Leo.

"Is Rory going to be okay?" I asked the detective.

"We don't know the full extent of his injuries. He has some broken bones and is severely dehydrated, but I think you found him in time," Detective Gupta said. "The medical team will make sure he gets all the treatment he needs."

"Thank goodness."

"Why didn't you search the zoo already?" Azalea asked the detective. "Why didn't you find him here before?"

"We did examine the zoo, but we didn't find him then," Detective Gupta replied. Her voice sounded uncharacteristically ashamed.

"Whitney must have had him in hiding when they searched. She didn't want him dead, just trapped, so she used the cage to keep him all for herself,"

I added. I appreciated Detective Gupta's work, but the county's team was small. I couldn't imagine they had enough manpower or resources to search everywhere more than once. I guessed that Whitney bet on that.

"How did you know it was Whitney?" the detective asked.

"Because it wasn't about the O'Doyle diary or the *Book of Kells*. It never was. Everyone else wanted the diary to find the missing covers, but that wasn't what Whitney cared about. She has always loved Rory—in her own twisted way. I think that when Azalea and Rory started divorce proceedings, Whitney had thought he would finally be available. Except then, she must have seen him with Tess O'Doyle."

Whitney had waited over twenty years to be with him, and suddenly, in her eyes, this young thing slides in and snatches him away. She was done. "In her mind, she didn't have anything left—no boyfriend, no career, nothing. She was ready to get revenge," I said. I imagined that when she saw them together, she snapped. She must have killed Tess in the cemetery and then kidnapped Rory, probably moving him here to avoid detection. Who would have imagined he would be trapped in the abandoned tiger cage?

"So, the calls and flowers continued after Rory disappeared?" Azalea asked.

"That must have been Whitney the entire time. She probably wanted to make you think he had been the one leaving you all those trinkets, so you would never try going back to him. I wouldn't be surprised if she was also the one who vandalized my car and your Carriage House. She wanted to scare me away," I said, putting the pieces together. "Being right next door, she knew a lot of what was going on and could easily slip in and out undetected."

"Then who won the diary in the auction?" the detective asked.

"Whitney," I said. "She must have found out about their plans to auction off the O'Doyle diary, and she made a ridiculous bid so she could meet them in the cemetery that night."

"But why did she use LEA as a username?" Azalea asked.

I sighed. "I think because it's your nickname. She knew Rory would see that, so she wanted to mess with him."

"She must have bid using your wi-fi so that the IP address would match too," the detective said.

"That makes sense," I replied.

"Our guest wi-fi was open, but I'll add a password," said Azalea. I had a feeling that was only the first of several security upgrades coming to the inn.

We followed Detective Gupta to the station to answer questions and give statements. Ruth headed back to update Orson and the Chronos Channel crew. I imagined they would be upset at having missed all the action, especially since I suspected they wouldn't find anything where the archaeologists were currently searching. To be honest, I still didn't know if the covers ever survived to Maryland, but I suspected that if they had, they were long gone by now.

Chapter Nineteen

The next morning, Azalea, Violet, and I went to the Purple Oyster for something to eat. Harmony welcomed us with open arms while Violet ran to the children's table in the corner to color pictures. "Oh, my sweeties, I heard what happened." Inside the café, it seemed everyone backed up to give us room, while still trying to eavesdrop however they could. I didn't care. I wanted to down buckets of coffee and eat mountains of food. Harmony led us to a table and whistled loudly through two fingers. The whole café turned to watch her. One of her staff hopped over, and she dictated a list of foods. I would not turn down her generosity.

Harmony bent next to me and said, "You are my hero, Juniper. Thank you for finding out the truth. For finding what happened to my darling Tess." She gave me a tight squeeze around my shoulders. "At least we've found a new family member."

"A new family member?"

"Well, I learned that Tess and Rory snuck around because they had discovered they were cousins. Rory is the long-lost son of my cousin, after having been put up for adoption as a baby. They all share a set of grandparents," she said with a beaming smile.

I looked confused. How did she know any of that?

"Oh, the DNA test," Azalea said.

"What test?" Harmony asked.

"I'd given Rory one for the holidays last year. Being adopted, he was exploring his family history," she explained. I remembered her telling Detective Gupta about the test when she interviewed us.

"Rory and Tess must have made a connection through the company," I said.

"Yes. I found a note from Tess in her work apron. She had been drafting it to me, but she hadn't finished it yet. It broke my heart to read it, but I'm so grateful I did. In the note, she explained that she had taken one of those tests and discovered about being connected to Rory," Harmony sighed loudly and long. "We had a fight on Friday night. You know how she had been gifted with such a beautiful voice. She wanted to go to New York to pursue her dreams, and I had told her not to do it. I had been worried about what would happen to her, that it wouldn't work, and that she would be hurt. I wish so much that I had encouraged her to go instead. After she connected with Rory, he convinced her to follow her dreams of being a musician. They were going to sell the cursed diary so that she could go for it."

No wonder Tess had been secretive in recent weeks. She must have trusted no one—not even her roommate and best friend Desiree—to keep her plan secret from her aunt. Rory must have been the only one who was part of the plan. Harmony must have been the person Tess was arguing with in the hallway on Friday night.

"But then why did he reach out to you, Juniper?" Azalea asked. I thought for a moment, remembering his email to me on Friday morning. Had that only been a few days ago? It felt like a lifetime away now.

"We'll have to ask him when he's better, but my gut instinct is that as the end of the auction drew near, he grew anxious about what they had done. If I were him, I would have been wondering things like, 'Was the diary real?' or 'Was what they were doing right?' It was an expensive risk."

"Wait, what about Leo?" Azalea asked.

"What about him?" Harmony asked with an uncertain look.

"Juniper said that he had offered her money to help her music career. Why didn't she accept that instead of selling your family's diary? He certainly has the finances to make that happen."

"Honestly, I had a lot to do with that. I really hated how Leo's family has been trying to destroy Rose Mallow. I may have said a few things I now regret."

"It wasn't your fault. I didn't know Tess well, but I suspect she wanted to pursue her dream her way and not have anyone footing the bill," I said.

Harmony nodded. "Yeah, that sounds like Tess. Besides, she knew how I had blamed the diary for her grandfather's death. She may have not wanted to tell me about getting rid of it, but she knew I wasn't a fan of keeping it."

Food arrived after that. Violet trotted over, and we all dug in. I ate too much and felt like I might need to be carted home. That thought stopped me in my tracks. When I thought about "home," I realized I didn't picture my row house in D.C. Instead, I thought of the Wildflower Inn and Rose Mallow. I hadn't realized how much I had missed it here.

"What?" Azalea asked, apparently noting my curious expression.

"How did you know?"

"Know what?"

"That you wanted to live in Rose Mallow," I said.

She laughed. "Rose Mallow has always been where my heart is. More than anywhere else. Partially because of Nana Z, partially because of Rory, and now because of Violet. I've never wanted to live anywhere else but here. I had always wanted to move here year-round when we were teens."

"I felt the opposite growing up. I wanted to explore the world," I replied.

"And you've done that. You've backpacked through Europe, you've taken train rides in Asia, you've hiked around South America. You've been to more places in a decade than I could imagine visiting in a lifetime," she said with a gentle smile.

"I thought I was an explorer at heart."

"You are," she interrupted.

"Well, yes, that may be true, but now I wonder if I wasn't trying to run away."

"Run away from what? From Rose Mallow?" She watched me curiously as I shrugged. "Whatever you may have been doing, what are you going to do now?"

"Honestly? I have no idea."

"I have full faith you'll figure it out," Azalea said.

When we returned to the Wildflower Inn, I noticed Cordelia Sullivan sitting on her porch in a rocking chair. "What do you think will happen to her?" I asked Azalea. I hoped that at least they had found a health aide before Whitney was arrested.

"I don't know," Azalea replied with a hint of sadness. "I want to help her, but I don't think she'll let me."

"It won't be easy living next door to her."

"It was hard enough before, but now?" She shook her head. I had a feeling that Azalea would try to work behind the scenes to help, especially if she could do things without being recognized, like having meals delivered or ensuring that a health aide appeared. She was so much like Nana Z sometimes.

At the Wildflower Inn, a nearby mob of people descended upon us. The Chronos Channel crew wanted an interview. "A few questions?" asked Ashley, already prepping her camera. The other members tried to fit us with lavalier mics. I looked at the wires and shook my head, thinking back to the amusement park.

"Not right now. We need a break." I put up my hands in a paltry attempt to shield myself from their cameras.

Ashley looked at her watch. "Okay, in an hour? It looks like you've been up all night. That'll give you time to wash up, too."

"I think it'd be more authentic if Juniper remains looking as frazzled and dirt-strewn," said one of the guys. I thought he was joking, but he looked completely serious.

"We could probably make her look more battered. Take some soil from the garden or something," added the other. All three nodded.

"What? No. I don't want to do any of that," I replied. Before I could get too testy, Keisha and Desiree interrupted to pull Violet into the inn while Clover danced around our feet. We closed the door on the TV crew, leaving them to their discussion on how best to make me look disheveled.

"I'm so glad you're okay," Keisha cried.

"We are too," Azalea replied as she cradled her daughter.

"And here, I have a present," said Keisha.

"Oh?"

She pulled a small box out of her back pocket. It was another phone. "When we heard you had lost your phone again, Desiree used your information to set up another one. Already connected to your number and ready to go."

"Thank you." I gave Keisha a big hug. I turned it on, just in time to be assaulted by another bevy of texts from Greyson, wondering where I was and threatening to fire me.

Then Leo appeared carrying a messenger bag, along with Ruth and Orson. Even a few of the archaeologists came with them. I tried to head over to Leo, but Orson caught me first and grabbed my hands. "My darling, darling Juniper. I am so incredibly sorry for the coarse and incredibly undeserved way that I treated you yesterday." He hung his head in shame. "I am not as in control of my drinking as I had thought. Ruth here has already found me the most wonderful of places to provide the help I require in regaining that control." He looked at her with a grateful smile. She dipped her head modestly.

"Thank you," I mouthed to her. She nodded.

"However, I hear you recognized the area we had been searching is likely not where the covers are?" Orson asked.

"I don't know for certain. I'm still uncertain whether they still exist—here in Maryland or anywhere else. Maybe now that the O'Doyle diary has been found, it will unlock future clues," I replied.

One of the archaeologists stepped in. "I heard it's not in great shape."

"That's true. I hope they're getting it preserved in an appropriate freezer until it can be assessed by a conservator. At least we have Ruth's photos," I said, turning towards her.

"Thank goodness for that," the archaeologist agreed. "Well, we'll at least finish the survey. Even if we don't find signs of the covers, we may find other important artifacts. That land goes back centuries, so who knows what discoveries we'll make there."

"Yes, that would be great," said Leo. "However, Juniper, if I may borrow you for a moment?" We wandered around the porch, away from the crowd, and to the back of the house into the garden. Although it was muggy, the day was not as hot as it had been. We found a bench amongst the hydrangeas to sit and talk. He dropped his messenger bag at his feet.

"I need to apologize," I said. Leo looked at me curiously. "I've ruined your sister's wig and clothes."

He batted away my concerns. "She'll be fine. I doubt she'll ever notice they were missing. Goodness knows how many she has." Leo then took my hands in his. "I am impressed by your knowledge and detective work with the manuscripts and books. Your passion is obvious, and I am amazed how you have seen things no one else has."

"Thanks, but it's not like I found the covers."

"Maybe not yet. But that's because you haven't had the right resources at your disposal. If anyone can find them, Juniper, it's you."

I felt my face flush. I wanted to push back, but I sat there and listened. We were still holding hands. I wondered if he was going to ask me on another date. I imagined the two of us working together to locate lost rare books and other cultural treasures. I thought about the photos he showed me of different grandparents who teamed up to explore the world. My heart beat quickly in my chest.

"I wanted to ask you if you would consider managing the collections at the Calverton Foundation," he said.

He pulled out a folder filled with papers from his messenger bag on the ground. "I know it's quick, but you're exceptional, and at the Calverton, we don't like to miss out on exceptional. In here, you'll find all the details about the job offer, including what it would entail, salary, benefits, and more."

"You want me to leave the Library of Congress?"

"I'd like you to at least consider the offer." He opened the folder and tapped at the salary. My mouth dropped. Compared to other librarians, I made a good salary and benefits working at the Library of Congress. Maybe not great compared to living costs in Washington, D.C., but it was enough for Clover and me. However, the amount I saw there was eye-popping, especially given how affordable living in Rose Mallow could be.

Taking this job meant I could be closer to my sister and niece. I could also help her with her money troubles. However, it also meant giving up the life I had carved out in D.C. Getting a job at the Library of Congress wasn't easy to accomplish, and taking this position meant changing my career trajectory in a big way.

I felt my phone buzz. I glanced down at it. Another text from Greyson. "Juniper, I need you to…" I had to laugh at his timing. Taking this job also meant I no longer had to bend to his every whim and demand. Being in a smaller organization also meant I'd be less of a cog.

"You want me to manage the collections?" I nearly whispered the words.

"You would become the first Executive Director of the Calverton Foundation Library and Archives," he replied.

I didn't know how to answer at first. Would this mean I would be the boss? No more dealing with someone who didn't know how to respect boundaries or emergencies?

"Who would I report to?"

"Well, I'd be your direct supervisor, I guess, and you'd report to the family board," he explained.

I sucked in my breath. "Can I have some time to think about this?"

"Of course," he replied. Then he tried to kiss my cheek. I pulled away. "Is everything okay?"

"Well." I didn't want to say it, but I needed to. "If I'm going to consider working for the Foundation and especially for you, we can't date. Not if you're going to be my boss. You're already concerned about how you and your family are perceived. I don't want to be perceived as working there because of you."

He looked surprised. "Fine. Then I retract the job offer." I felt blown back until he laughed. "I'm joking. I promise. Look, I'll happily take you as a colleague or however you want to be here. How about instead of a kiss, a handshake?"

"Of course." We shook hands.

"Uh, excuse me?" I looked up to see Detective Gupta and Deputy Torres arrive. "Is this a bad time?"

I stood up and futilely wiped at my clothes. I wasn't sure why I bothered. "Not at all. What can I do to help you?"

Detective Gupta said, "I came to apologize. To you and your sister."

"Where's Azalea?" Deputy Torres interrupted. He looked so excited. Then, he seemed to remember that he was still in uniform and tried to take on a more stoic expression. I couldn't help but chuckle lightly.

"I'm right here." Azalea came out with yet another one of Nana Z's recipes. I recognized its scent immediately: tzimmes cake. Much like a carrot cake, it included a wealth of flavors, like orange zest, ginger, cinnamon, and cloves. However, it didn't just have carrots in the batter but apples and sweet potatoes as well. Tzimmes cake was one of my favorite treats. "Trying to get around to everyone."

"I think people are here to show you hospitality, not the other way around," I said. Azalea shrugged and continued passing out slices of tzimmes cake. Deputy Torres took one, but everyone else politely declined, although I could see them watching the cake go by with jealousy. "Detective Gupta and Deputy Torres were looking for you."

"Oh?" Azalea asked.

"I wanted to apologize for pulling you in. Accusing you of being involved," Detective Gupta said.

"I understand. I'm glad you found the actual killer and saved Rory," she said. The amazing thing about Azalea was that I was pretty sure she meant every word. I wasn't so sure I'd be as forgiving at having been considered a criminal, even if it was just briefly.

"That was all because of your sister," Deputy Torres said. I smiled gratefully.

"And I'd like to debrief. I've gathered you two have put together more of the missing pieces," the detective added.

"Of course, of course," replied Azalea.

We thanked our well-wishers and eventually, they all drifted away. Azalea and I led the detectives to the kitchen, where we caught them up on what we had learned at the Purple Oyster. Deputy Torres spent most of the conversation sneaking glances at Azalea. She exchanged a few back with her soft smile. I wondered if they had started dating yet. Then I thought about Rory. As much as it warmed my heart to see her excited about someone, I knew I needed to tell her what he had said in the tiger cage.

It wasn't until much later in the day that I finally had a chance to pull Azalea aside. "Have you heard any updates about Rory?" I asked. We headed out to the inn's wraparound porch and found a swinging bench to sit on that looked out at the Chesapeake Bay.

"Going to the hospital in an hour to check on him," she said. "Violet's working on drawing some pictures for him."

"You should know that when I was at the Zoo, Rory thought I was you. He was not in good shape. I didn't correct him," I said. Azalea nodded. "He kept apologizing, saying the divorce was his fault. He said he was sorry he wasn't there for you when you needed him." I took a breath. Azalea's eyes welled with tears. "He wants to come home and work things out with you."

"Oh, Rory," she said softly. Then she looked up at me. "It wasn't his fault. Not really. I had a hard time adjusting to the baby and the house, and Nana Z... I really struggled. Rory did everything he could for me."

"What are you going to do?" I watched the waters of the Bay drift across to the horizon.

She shrugged. "I don't know if I'm still in love with him." She stopped swinging on the bench. "I will always love him in some way, but I don't know what I feel right now." She wrung her hands as she spoke.

"What about Deputy Torres?"

She shrugged. "I don't know about that either. But I definitely feel something for him. Did you know I never kissed another man before Rory? I have a lot to figure out."

"You will," I assured her. "Start by going to the hospital. That's a good first step. And I'll be here for you, however you need."

"You're going to stay?" Azalea asked, sounding surprised.

"I'm thinking about it. I'm not sure yet. Well, I'm sure about one thing."

"What's that?"

"I might stay in Rose Mallow, but maybe not in the Carriage House," I said with a shudder, thinking about the towers of boxes inside. Besides, it was going to become a more permanent home for Azalea and Violet.

"You know, there's something I found in there that I wanted to show you," Azalea said. I lifted my eyebrows, curious about what it could be. She disappeared and returned carrying a hand-carved wooden box. When she opened it up, I saw the box was nearly overflowing with leather-bound notebooks. "These were Nana Z's. You already saw her watercolor journals, but these were her diaries. I've started looking through them. If you move back here, or at least visit, I could use your help. If you're willing," she said.

"Of course." I pulled one out gingerly and looked through the first few pages. I recognized her scribble immediately, and, of course, there was a small pen and ink sketch of Azalea and me as kids playing in the garden. I could see how much love and care had gone into the drawing. Tears welled in my eyes. My decision was made because I knew I was truly home.

A Note from the Author

While the O'Doyle diary and its map in this story are not real, the *Book of Kells* very much is. Scholars believe that this exquisite early example of an illustrated Gospel book was created around the 9th century in the British Isles. This is in part based on the type of artwork used in the 680 pages of *Kells*. The book is a prime example of Hiberno-Saxon or Insular art. Hiberno refers to the Hibernians, or the Irish, and their interactions with the Anglo-Saxons of southern England. This style is characterized by interlacing decoration and the combination of Irish curvilinear forms with Saxon's abstract patterns, including elaborate intertwined animals. *Kells* is a true highlight of this artistic style with its ornate swirls, living figures, and, of course, Celtic knots and patterns, all painted in vibrant colors that command your attention.

No one knows where *Kells* was created, but many scholars believe the manuscript was made, at least in part, at the Iona Abbey on the island of Iona, off the western coast of Scotland. At some point, the book was brought to the Abbey of Kells in county Meath, Ireland. Some think the book was finished there, while other scholars believe it was brought already complete to Kells.

That the book survived is surprising and miraculous. The Kells Abbey was pillaged by Vikings many times. It's in 1007 that we see the first reference to the *Book of Kells* in the Annals of Ulster, describing how "the great Gospel of Columkille (a reference to Saint Columba)" had been "wickedly stolen during the night from the western sacristy of the great stone church at Cenannas on account of its wrought shrine." The wrought shrine is a reference to its bejeweled cover. The manuscript inside the book was amazingly discovered several months later "under a sod" but missing its ornate cover, which was never seen again.

Crime and Parchment takes the conceit that the cover, or possibly an actual shrine, was recovered and hidden away for safekeeping. Indeed, the book itself remained in Kells until 1654 during the English Civil War. A few years earlier, King Charles I had dissolved Parliament, who had been trying to curb his power. They fought back, and he soon lost to the armies of the English and Scottish parliaments. After Charles' execution in 1649, Oliver Cromwell became the ruler of a new, short-lived republic of England. Because Cromwell's cavalry stayed at the church in Kells, the book was moved to Dublin for safekeeping. It became part of Trinity College in Dublin in 1661 and has remained there through the present day. I've had the lovely fortune to visit them in person. The artistry is astonishing. Unable to visit *Kells* in person? Explore them online at https://www.tcd.ie/visitors/book-of-kells/.

Crime and Parchment also uses the conceit that there was a plan to send *Kells* and their long-missing covers to Maryland during this chaotic period. Unlike other colonies, Maryland was created as a safe haven for Catholic people by Cecil Calvert, an English nobleman who was the first Proprietor of the "Province of Maryland." Cecil was an English Roman Catholic in an otherwise Anglican country, so it was important to him that the colony was a place of religious tolerance. Although he never came to Maryland, he sent his younger brother, Leonard Calvert, who was the first governor of the colony. The Calverton family - and especially Leonard and Cecil Calverton - are named in memory of the Calverts.

Join My Newsletter

Join my newsletter list at www.daphnesilver.com to get the free short story, "A Midsummer's Night Scheme!" A rum runner's mansion, a 1623 copy of Shakespeare's "First Folio," and a performance of a *Midsummer's Night Dream* set in a speakeasy... what more could a history loving librarian want? Juniper Blume had simply planned a fun night out with her sister Azalea. She certainly didn't expect to stumble upon a rare books' puzzle in a classic locked room style mystery. Will she figure out the truth before the final curtain drops?

Acknowledgements

Thank you to:
  * Level Best editor Shawn Reilly Simmons and everyone at Level Best
  * Blackstone Audio and my narrator Barrie Kreinik
  * Agent Cindy Bullard of Birch Literary
  * My writing group: Cathy Wiley, Debbi Mack, Marcia Talley, Mary Ellen Hughes, Becky Hutchison, Shaun Taylor Bevins, and Rosalie Spielman
  * Sisters in Crime, especially the Chesapeake Chapter
  * The Chessie Chapter Zoom crew
  * Korina Moss and Sherry Harris
  * My mom
  * Early readers: Regina Sokas, Lynley Herbert, and Jobi Zink
  * Jenny Kane
  * Kristen Harbeson
  * My husband and son

About the Author

Daphne Silver is the author of the Rare Books Cozy Mystery series. She's worked more than twenty years in museums and has the great fortune of being married to a librarian. When she's not writing, she's drawing and painting. She lives in Maryland with her family. Although she's not much of a baker, she won't ever turn down a sweet lokshen kugel.

SOCIAL MEDIA HANDLES:
    www.facebook.com/daphnesilverbooks
    www.instagram.com/daphnesilverbooks

AUTHOR WEBSITE:
    www.daphnesilver.com

Also by Daphne Silver

Writing as Lauren R. Silberman:

The Jewish Community of Baltimore (Arcadia Publishing, 2007)

Wicked Baltimore: Charm City Sin and Scandal (History Press, 2011)

Wild Women of Maryland: Grit and Gumption in the Free State (History Press, 2015)

Chesapeake Crimes: Storm Warning (2016)

Fish or Cut Bait: A Guppy Anthology (2015) (as Lauren Moffett)